EARTH, SEA & STARS

For William, Cate,
Alex and Miranda
~ IO

For Ariadna,
the heroine of a thousand
and one fairy tales
~ AS

Caterpillar Books
An imprint of the Little Tiger Group
1 Coda Studios, 189 Munster Road, London SW6 6AW
Imported into the EEA by Penguin Random House Ireland,
Morrison Chambers, 32 Nassau Street, Dublin D02 YH68
www.littletiger.co.uk
First published in Great Britain 2022
Text by Isabel Otter
Text copyright © 2022 Caterpillar Books Ltd
Illustrations copyright © 2022 Ana Sender
Map and compass images courtesy of www.shutterstock.com
A CIP catalogue record for this book is available from the British Library
All rights reserved • Printed in China
ISBN: 978-1-83891-395-3 • CPB/1400/1966/0921
10 9 8 7 6 5 4 3 2 1

The Forest Stewardship Council® (FSC®) is an international,
non-governmental organisation dedicated to promoting responsible
management of the world's forests. FSC® operates a system of forest
certification and product labelling that allows consumers to identify
wood and wood-based products from well-managed forests and
other controlled sources.

For more information about the FSC®,
please visit their website at www.fsc.org

EARTH, SEA & STARS

RETOLD BY
ISABEL OTTER

ILLUSTRATED BY
ANA SENDER

LiTTLE TiGER
LONDON

Contents

Story Map

6

The Corn Girl
North America

**Searching
for Summer**
North America

The Banyan Tree
Tahiti

**The Fox and
the Armadillo**
Argentina

**Stairway
to the
Stars**
England

Selkie Island
Scotland

**The
Discontented
Pine Tree**
Denmark

**The Deer's
Antlers**
Greece

**King and
Queen of
the Skies**
Nigeria

Finding Fire
*Democratic
Republic of
the Congo*

N

W   E

S

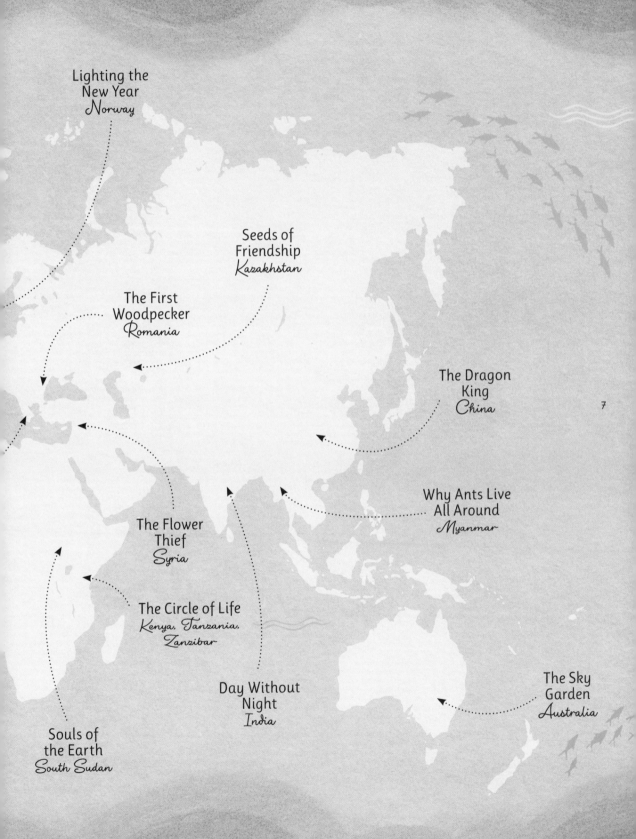

Lighting the
New Year
Norway

Seeds of
Friendship
Kazakhstan

The First
Woodpecker
Romania

The Dragon
King
China

Why Ants Live
All Around
Myanmar

The Flower
Thief
Syria

The Circle of Life
*Kenya, Tanzania,
Zanzibar*

Day Without
Night
India

The Sky
Garden
Australia

Souls of
the Earth
South Sudan

7

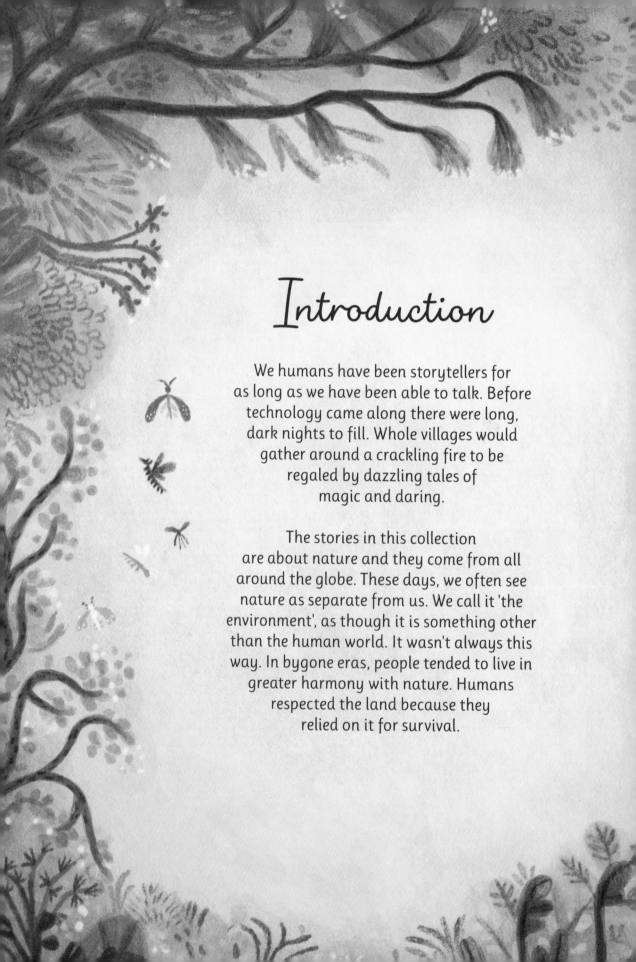

Introduction

We humans have been storytellers for
as long as we have been able to talk. Before
technology came along there were long,
dark nights to fill. Whole villages would
gather around a crackling fire to be
regaled by dazzling tales of
magic and daring.

The stories in this collection
are about nature and they come from all
around the globe. These days, we often see
nature as separate from us. We call it 'the
environment', as though it is something other
than the human world. It wasn't always this
way. In bygone eras, people tended to live in
greater harmony with nature. Humans
respected the land because they
relied on it for survival.

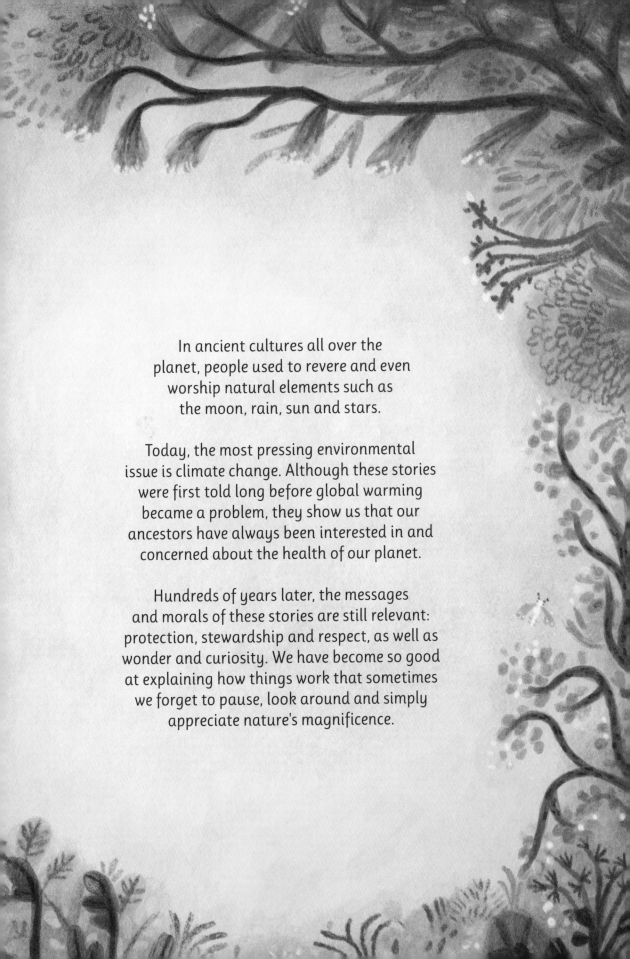

In ancient cultures all over the
planet, people used to revere and even
worship natural elements such as
the moon, rain, sun and stars.

Today, the most pressing environmental
issue is climate change. Although these stories
were first told long before global warming
became a problem, they show us that our
ancestors have always been interested in and
concerned about the health of our planet.

Hundreds of years later, the messages
and morals of these stories are still relevant:
protection, stewardship and respect, as well as
wonder and curiosity. We have become so good
at explaining how things work that sometimes
we forget to pause, look around and simply
appreciate nature's magnificence.

THE DRAGON KING
A story from China

There was once a young man called Li Ching whose greatest wish was to become a wise teacher. He heard tell of a scholar who worked at the top of Dragon Gate Mountain and determined to become one of his pupils.

Li Ching set off on his mission by foot. It was high summer, and the ground was parched, cracked and hard as bone. The countryside had been suffering a serious drought for the last three years. The crops lay withered and dead in the fields, the flowers had wilted and even the trees seemed to droop. It saddened Li Ching terribly to see his beloved countryside transformed into a barren wasteland.

As he was walking, Li Ching passed a Dragon King temple with a large crowd of people outside. The Dragon King was the god of rain, and the local people felt aggrieved that he had not answered their prayers. Li Ching watched as an angry mob came out of the temple carrying a statue of the Dragon King. They attempted to dump the statue outside in the heat to make him suffer, but various people intervened and a great hullabaloo began. *What misery this drought is causing*, thought Li Ching as he hurried on past.

Li Ching was so busy worrying about the drought that he forgot to concentrate on where he was going. Dusk began to fall, and Li Ching suddenly realised that he was lost. Ahead of him was a mountain that he didn't recognise. He had come too far now to turn back. There was nothing for it but to climb the mountain and hope to find an inn before it got too dark.

After some time, Li Ching found himself in a deep forest. He was hopelessly lost now and at his wits' end – every twist and turn led him further into the maze of trees.

Li Ching was about to curl up under a tree and wait for morning when he noticed a flickering light ahead. Overjoyed, he ran towards it and came upon a house. The dwelling stood alone in a small clearing. Strangely, there was no path leading to it. Something about the house made Li Ching uneasy but he swallowed his nerves; he needed a place to stay.

Li Ching knocked, and a shrunken old woman answered the door. He begged her to let him stay for the night and warily she agreed. The old woman led him into a small room and laid out a sleeping mat.

"I'm sorry that I have nothing more to offer you," she said humbly.

"This suits me perfectly," replied Li Ching.

As soon as the old woman had left, Li Ching collapsed onto his sleeping mat. He fell into a deep slumber, but it wasn't long before he was woken by an urgent knocking at the front door. Creeping over to the window, Li Ching saw the old lady letting a young boy into the house, and he overheard everything they said.

"Granny, I have come straight from heaven! I was playing up there and minding my own business when the Emperor God himself gave me an urgent instruction for my father! He is ordered to go up to heaven before dawn to summon the rain."

"Oh no! What are we to do?" lamented the old woman. "Your father is away and won't be back for several days. Dawn will break in just a few hours!"

Li Ching shook his head in disbelief. *I am in the house of the Dragon King god himself, and these two must be Dragon Mother and Little Dragon. The people's prayers have been answered!* But then the door slammed. Little Dragon was walking away, yelling, "I will tell the Emperor god that my father cannot make the rain tonight."

"No!" shouted Li Ching, running out after him. "Please – the drought has ruined the land and the people are desperate.

There must be something we can do!"

"Who are you?" asked Little Dragon in surprise.

"Quiet!" said Dragon Mother. "I've had an idea..."

Before he knew what was happening, Li Ching found himself dressed up in the crown and robes of the Dragon King.

"You look just the part!" said Dragon Mother. "When you arrive in heaven, you must wave this black flag in order to command the gods of wind, thunder and lightning. As long as you have the flag, no one will question you."

Dragon Mother led Li Ching outside, where Little Dragon was waiting next to a beautiful white stallion. The boy presented Li Ching with a water vase made from white jade, and a branch of willow.

"You will use these to make the rain, but don't forget – one drop in heaven goes a long way on Earth," Dragon Mother said. "Listen to Little Dragon. He will tell you how many drops to scatter. Now, climb onto the white horse. He will take you up to heaven."

Li Ching climbed on nervously, pulling Little Dragon with him, and the stallion soared upwards! The world looked so neat and orderly from above: the square fields, ridged mountains and curling rivers that stretched all the way into the sea.

"Here we are," said Little Dragon.

They had landed in heaven. Li Ching waved his black flag and the weather gods assembled. As soon as he had uttered his commands, they dispersed again. The god of wind blew stray clouds into an enormous bank. Gathered like this, the clouds blotted out the light of the sun, and darkness fell on the land below.

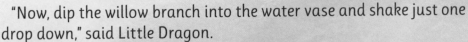

"Now, dip the willow branch into the water vase and shake just one drop down," said Little Dragon.

Li Ching did as he was told and then made his final order to the gods of lightning and thunder. A blinding flash of light streamed through the clouds, followed by an almighty crack and a deafening growl of thunder. It was as though the clouds had been ripped apart – a deluge of water fell from the sky and onto the thirsty ground below.

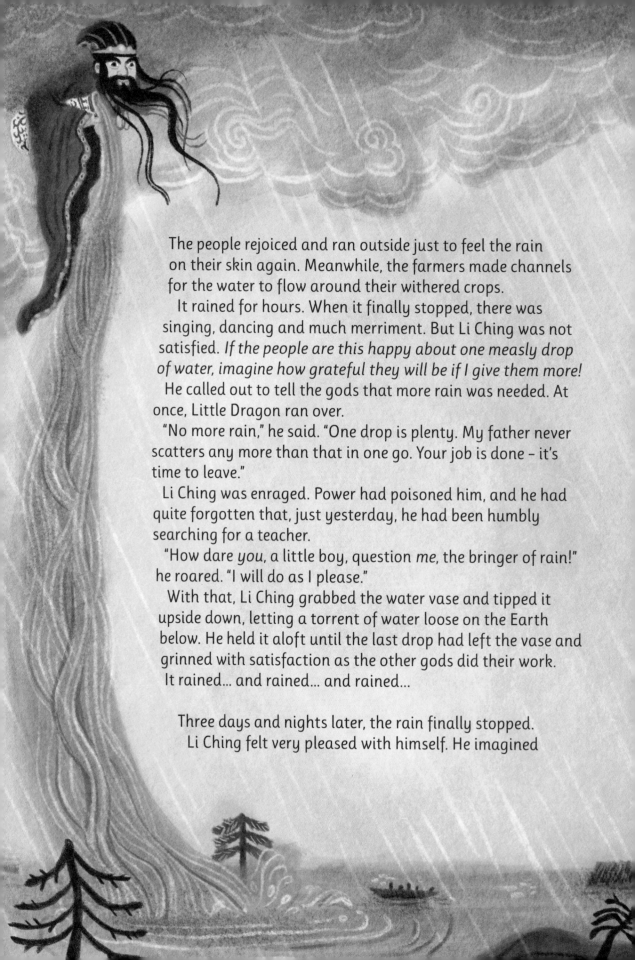

The people rejoiced and ran outside just to feel the rain
on their skin again. Meanwhile, the farmers made channels
for the water to flow around their withered crops.

It rained for hours. When it finally stopped, there was
singing, dancing and much merriment. But Li Ching was not
satisfied. *If the people are this happy about one measly drop
of water, imagine how grateful they will be if I give them more!*

He called out to tell the gods that more rain was needed. At
once, Little Dragon ran over.

"No more rain," he said. "One drop is plenty. My father never
scatters any more than that in one go. Your job is done – it's
time to leave."

Li Ching was enraged. Power had poisoned him, and he had
quite forgotten that, just yesterday, he had been humbly
searching for a teacher.

"How dare *you*, a little boy, question *me*, the bringer of rain!"
he roared. "I will do as I please."

With that, Li Ching grabbed the water vase and tipped it
upside down, letting a torrent of water loose on the Earth
below. He held it aloft until the last drop had left the vase and
grinned with satisfaction as the other gods did their work.

It rained... and rained... and rained...

Three days and nights later, the rain finally stopped.
Li Ching felt very pleased with himself. He imagined

how grateful the people on Earth would be and how they would worship him!

It was time to leave heaven. Li Ching got onto the white stallion and they made their way down. As they got closer to the ground, Li Ching gasped in horror. Everything below them was submerged in water. A flood had swept over the land and turned it into the sea!
The mountains were the only places safe from the flood. Li Ching could see crowds of people snaking up the mountain tracks with possessions piled on their heads.

   The horse dropped him off at the top of Dragon Gate Mountain, and Li Ching hung his head in shame and wept bitter tears.

   An old man came past and asked Li Ching why he was crying. He explained everything and the old man introduced himself as Wen Chung-tzu – the very scholar whom Li Ching had set out to find in the first place.

   "You have learnt a harsh lesson today, my boy, but don't be disheartened. Perhaps you meant well, but remember that goodwill alone is not always enough. You allowed a taste of power to overthrow your sense and ignored the advice of a friend. We must think carefully about the impact of our actions, even if our intentions are honest."

   "It seems I have a lot to learn..." said Li Ching remorsefully.

   "The journey begins here," smiled Wen Chung-tzu as they entered the scholar's temple.

THE CIRCLE OF LIFE
A Swahili story (Kenya, Tanzania, Zanzibar)

One sunny afternoon, an enormous python emerged out of the scrub. It was larger than the length of two men and its scales had a beautiful brown and gold mottled pattern that glinted in the sunlight. Reptiles take their energy from the heat of the sun and this snake was no exception. He had not eaten for many days and was very hungry. But before he could hunt, the python needed to absorb the magical golden rays that would revitalise him. He slithered out from underneath a bush, and his scales gleamed as he coiled his body into a comfortable position. The python opened his jaws wide in order to taste the air.

It was peaceful and quiet in the clearing, and the snake congratulated himself on finding such a good spot. All of a sudden, he stiffened, and his forked tongue flicked back and forth. He had picked up the acrid scent of smoke on the air. *Hunters must be burning the scrub to force the animals out*, he thought to himself.

Quick as a blink, the snake glided out of the clearing towards the land of a farmer, calling, "Help! Help! The hunters are burning the shrubs and bushes of my home, and they mean to kill me."

The farmer rushed out but stopped in his tracks at the sight of the enormous python. He began to back away, trembling all over with fear.

"Do not be afraid – I mean you no harm. All I ask is that you help me to hide," said the snake.

The farmer was a kindhearted soul. He loved animals and always did his best to rescue those in need. Swallowing his fright, he picked up a sack and beckoned the snake inside. As soon as the tip of the snake's tail had disappeared into the sack, two hunters rushed onto the scene.

"Farmer, we are looking for a huge python, the biggest of its kind for miles around. Have you seen it?"

"Why no, I'm afraid I haven't," said the farmer.

The hunters caressed their spears and stepped closer.

"Then why do we see snake tracks leading from the scrubland and straight into your field?"

"Are there? My goodness, I'd better go inside at once. I'm terrified of snakes!" said the farmer.

He turned on his heel, rushed into his hut and barred the door. He peeked through the window at the hunters as they prowled around his fields. Finding nothing, they eventually slunk away, and the farmer breathed a relieved sigh.

He opened the sack and told the snake that the coast was clear. To his horror, the snake slid up his legs and coiled around his middle, squeezing tighter and tighter as he went.

"What are you doing?" the farmer gasped. "I just saved you from those hunters!"

"That is true, but nevertheless I am very hungry, and eating you will keep me going for a long time," hissed the python.

The farmer tried to prise the snake off, but it was no good. He was much too strong for him.

"Wait a second," cried the farmer. "You can eat me, but first you must repay me for saving your life. It is only fair."

The python relaxed his hold a little.

"Yes, you are right. Go on then, Farmer – what would you like me to do for you before I eat you?"

"You must agree to let others decide whether you should eat me."

"Fine," said the snake, sliding down from the farmer's body. "Come along, then. Let's ask this banana plant."

The snake and the farmer approached the plant and explained what was happening.

"Surely you agree that the snake should have mercy on me," pleaded the farmer.

"What do you humans know of mercy? Do you show mercy in cutting down every bunch of bananas I ever grow? Are you merciful when you chop off my lovely leaves in order to thatch the roof of your house? No! You think only of yourselves. I say the snake should eat you!"

"Good," said the snake.

"Wait!" shouted the farmer desperately. "Let us ask the bee."

The bee listened patiently and shook her head.

"I'm sorry, Farmer, but I agree with Snake. Humans do not deserve the compassion of animals. My family and I spend months making honey and then along come people with smoking torches to force us out of our hive. They take all of our honey and give us not a word of thanks in return. Snake, you are welcome to him."

"Thank you," grinned the snake, opening his jaws wide.

"Please! Let us ask one more animal!" wailed the farmer.

"Very well," said the snake.

An oryx stood grazing nearby, and the farmer approached to explain his plight.

"You are my last hope. Will you tell the snake to spare me?"

The oryx looked at him with surprise and disdain.

"Of course I won't tell the snake to spare you! Humans kill us without a second thought. I have seen people hunt my kind when they did not even need to eat. They did it for sport, for fun. I'm sorry, Farmer, but it's perfectly fair for the snake to eat you."

Aghast, the farmer sank to the ground. Just then, a voice floated out from a nearby acacia tree.

"This is the circle of life. Every creature must eat to survive. You cannot blame the snake for his desire to live. Invisible threads connect all of us in this world. Humans must not forget their place in the fine balance. You are animals, too!"

The python and farmer looked up to see a large baboon.

"So, Baboon, you, too, agree that I should eat the farmer?" asked the snake.

"Not so fast. First, show me exactly how this all came about. Is that the sack? I do not believe that a sack so small could hold a snake as large and fine as you."

"Well, I shall show you," said the python as he slithered into the sack.

"What happened next?" asked the baboon.

"I closed the sack with this rope," replied the farmer.

"Show me," the baboon said.

The farmer obliged and closed the sack with the snake inside.

"Well, Farmer," said the baboon,
"I wonder if you feel any differently after
your conversations with the plants and
animals. It appears that the fate of this
snake once again rests with you."

THE BANYAN TREE
A story from Tahiti

Ru and Hina were brother and sister gods. They lived happily on the beautiful island of Raiatea, but their spirits longed for adventure. Hina and Ru decided to explore all four of Earth's corners in their canoe, Little Flower. They marvelled at rushing rivers and waterfalls, mountains and deep ravines, forests, deserts and ice caps. They watched volcanoes erupt, avalanches tumble and encountered great storms with waves that reared up as tall as trees.

The siblings paddled with whales that glided gently alongside their canoe, nudging playfully at the edge. They saw shoals of flying fish, their scales glittering in the sun as they leapt out of the water. Turtles floated lazily in the ocean's currents above coral reefs that glowed like rainbow jewels beneath the waves.

   Either Ru or Hina would paddle while the other sat in the front, watching for land. Every island they passed and every creature they saw, they took note of. In this way, Ru and Hina began to map the Earth and all of its many birds and beasts.

After a long and fruitful journey, Hina and Ru returned to the island of Raiatea. At first, they were happy to be home.

Hina busied herself making a cloth called *tapa* from the breadfruit tree. She stripped off sections of bark and spooned out the soft inner parts. After drying the bark, Hina beat it for a while until she had long, thin strips that could be glued together into a large sheet. She painted the sheets with intricate patterns and hung them all over the island.

She was outwardly happy, yet inside Hina yearned for further adventures. Her voyage around the world had given her a taste for exploration, and having mapped the Earth, Hina was ready to journey into space. She felt a strong pull towards the moon. Each night, when she gazed up at its benign face, she thought she heard it whispering.

"Hina," the moon said. "Come to me."

Hina explained to Ru that she had been called to the moon. Though unwilling to say goodbye, he knew that there was no use trying to dissuade stubborn Hina once she had made up her mind. That night, Hina climbed into Little Flower and set off alone. She paddled her way into the sky, through the clouds and out into the sea of stars. As soon as the canoe entered the realm of space, Hina was greeted with perfect silence. She paddled on towards the moon and started to notice long, twisted shadows running over the moon's face like dark veins.

Eventually, Hina arrived, and the canoe crunched onto the moon's surface. She realised that the shadows were roots – the roots of a banyan tree! This wonderful old tree had taken over the whole cratered surface. If you've ever seen a banyan tree, you will know that its roots grow above ground, making it seem as though the tree has hundreds of trunks. It was the most glorious sight that Hina had ever seen. The tree gave off a gentle moonglow, and Hina felt a sense of calm and belonging. She had found her home.

Hina built a tree house and continued to make her *tapa* cloth, which was now even more beautiful because it radiated moonglow like the tree itself.

One day, a large fig dropped onto Hina's head and startled her. Looking up, she saw a grey-green fruit dove that flapped its wings in welcome. Hina called the animal by name.

"Come to me, U'upa."

The dove flew down at once, and from then on, Hina was never lonely as she had the chatter of U'upa for company.

Hina was enjoying her new life on the moon, but she hadn't forgotten her brother on Earth. One day, she asked U'upa to take down a beakful of figs so that Ru would be able to grow a tree of his very own.

The dove set off bravely. He threaded his way past the stars and planets, keeping his beady eyes fixed on the green and blue marble of Earth.

Just as U'upa had soared through Earth's curtain of clouds, a magnificent frigate bird appeared out of nowhere. Its throat pouch was puffed out, and its hooked beak was ready to attack. The frigate bird wanted to steal the figs from U'upa so that it could have the glory of bringing the banyan seeds to Earth itself. But Hina was watching, and she blew with all her might from the moon. A gust of wind rushed through space to Earth and blasted the frigate bird away. The path was clear, and U'upa was able to land on Raiatea with his beakful of figs.

Ru received the gift of figs and sowed the seeds, which grew into huge banyan trees. Hina smiled down from the moon.

These trees continue to prosper and bring fruit to all the islands of Polynesia. On a clear night, be sure to look for the shadows of the banyan trees on the face of the moon. To this day, Hina watches over those who travel by night and keeps them safe. If you're lucky, you might even see her smiling down upon you.

WHY ANTS LIVE ALL AROUND
A story from Myanmar

*L*ion was the king of the animals. As king, he liked to treat his subjects by offering up a wonderful banquet every month. Of all the animals, Ant was always last to arrive because of her very short legs. She just couldn't move as fast as the others.

When Ant arrived, the other animals had already started the banquet. They hooted with laughter as Ant took her place.

"A little late aren't you, Ant?"

"The party's started Ant – what took you so long?" they jeered.

Even King Lion joined in with the teasing.

"What does it matter when Ant arrives. She's so small that nobody notices her anyway!"

Ant was so embarrassed and upset that she crept away from the banquet table. She could hear the other animals laughing and making jokes as she made her slow way home. *Lion's right,* Ant thought sadly. *Nobody even realised that I'd left the banquet. From now on, I shall stay out of everybody's way and keep to myself.*

Ant went back to her nest and for a while was undisturbed. Then, one morning, King Lion woke with a terrible pain in his ear. He tried to ease it by rubbing, but his sharp claws only made it worse.

"Somebody help!" roared Lion. "Something has crawled into my ear and is biting me. I can feel it. Somebody get it out NOW!"

The animals quivered with fright. They all lived in fear of Lion's rages.

"We need someone with a long beak," they said. "We must call the birds."

One by one, the birds came and pecked at Lion's ear, trying to find the intruder, but none could reach in far enough.

"The beaks didn't work, so we must try a creature with a long tongue," said the animals.

They rushed to find the anteater. But his tongue wasn't long enough to reach the source of pain, either.

"Monkeys are good at nit picking," said the animals. "Perhaps one of them can help Lion."

A monkey was found and she tried her very best, but she too was unable to help. Meanwhile, Lion was becoming more and more irate.

Suddenly, Rabbit had an idea and bounded off. Where do you think Rabbit went? Why, straight to Ant's nest!

"Ant, are you there?" Rabbit called urgently. "Lion needs your help!"

It had not escaped Ant's notice that none of the animals had visited her or apologised for the scene at the banquet. Of course, now that they needed something it was quite different... Ant sighed. She was not a bitter animal, so she crawled out of her nest.

"Get on my back. It will be quicker," said Rabbit.

Ant did so, and they raced back to Lion's lair. The king was lying in a rather pathetic manner, howling in pain and misery while surrounded by worried animals. When they saw that Rabbit had brought Ant with him, the animals began to snigger.

"What could that little mite possibly do to help King Lion?"

But Lion silenced them angrily. He was ready to accept help from any quarter.

Quickly and quietly, Ant scuttled up Lion's leg, through his mane and right into his ear. She travelled all the way along his ear canal and easily found the root of the problem. A small biting worm was happily burrowing its way further and further into Lion's ear. Ant grabbed the worm in her mouth and tugged it out. The worm wriggled away, and Lion's torment was cured.

"Ant, you have saved me from pain and madness. I will grant you anything you wish. What shall it be?"

"My greatest wish is that I should be able to live wherever I please, Your Majesty," said Ant.

"Well, so be it!" said the king.

From that day on, Ant roamed about wherever she liked and made her home in many places. And this is why, wherever you look, almost anywhere in the world, you will find ants living there.

LIGHTING THE NEW YEAR
A story from Norway

It was New Year's Eve, and a little boy called Hans was on his way to visit his grandparents. He wore brand-new boots and a smart matching red waistcoat and hat. In his knapsack, Hans carried a twelfth-night candle and a small Christmas cake.

As Hans walked, snow began to drift down gently. It was hard going, but as he reached the woods, he remembered that there was a shortcut. *As long as I stick to the path, all will be well,* Hans thought.

However, before long, the soft flakes had turned into a raging blizzard, and a thick white carpet obscured the path entirely. Hans found himself deep in the woods with no idea of which way to go. Snow continued to fall, and there was no moon to cast a friendly glow.

Poor Hans was blue with cold when he noticed a faint light glimmering through the trees. He picked himself up and stumbled towards it. The light was being cast by a crackling fire. Around the edge of it sat twelve robed men and women in perfect stillness and silence.

Each of them wore a different adornment – ears of corn, a wreath of spring flowers, a headdress of icicles. All twelve seemed lost in thought.

Hans felt afraid, but the cold got the better of him, and he edged towards the warm flames, holding out his chilled hands to thaw. As he approached, a woman with a crown of ice raised an eyebrow and surveyed him.

29

"Hello, little one. Do you know who we are?" she asked.
"I think I do," replied Hans bravely.
"Well, go on... who are we?"
Hans began to recite the verses that he had been taught long ago by his mother:

*January brings a frozen glaze,
icicles and shortened days.*

*In February frost arrives,
its chilling grip a cold surprise.*

*In March the snow begins to thaw
and spring is opening her door.*

*In April mild showers fall;
new-grown shoots are standing tall.*

*In May the birds sing in the sky
and blossom fills the trees on high.*

*In June soft sunshine bathes the earth;
the boys and girls are full of mirth.*

*In July the summer smiles;
flowers bloom in cheerful styles.*

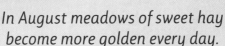

In August meadows of sweet hay
become more golden every day.

September's boughs are full of fruits
when autumn starts to put down roots.

In October, harvest starts;
food fills barrows, sacks and carts.

November brings a bitter chill;
the wind howls with its piercing shrill.

December's snow is here to stay;
the Advent candle lights the way.

31

"Very good, Hans. Yes, we know you too," said Sister December with
a smile, for the robed figures were none other than the twelve months
of the year.

"The old year is about to end, and we need your help to welcome in
the new year. Look how low the fire has become. You must climb inside
the cloak of Brother January. You will watch as the new year is handed
down from the moon and stars. Then, you must fetch us new fire with
your candle before the old fire goes out. When you have done this, I
will pass the staff to Brother January."

Hans thought he could hear the sound of tiny tinkling bells coming
from deep in the ground, but he couldn't be sure... He slipped under
the cloak of Brother January and entered the realm of the fairies.

Hans could see the moon and stars, but he was looking at them
through a gauzy veil. All sorts of magical beings were trotting around.
Hans saw brownies and goblins, pixies and gnomes. They looked as
though they were on their way to a feast. The brownies carried little
acorn baskets filled with nuts. The gnomes had sacks woven out of

grass and were busily stuffing tiny mushrooms inside. The pixies carried sweet nectar in foxgloves and the goblins pulled leaves behind them, piled with delicious berries. Each fairy held a tiny lantern, and a happy chattering and chirruping could be heard above all of the industry.

Hans watched in wonder and nearly forgot about the job he had been sent to do. He looked down and noticed that his candle was already being lit by a tiny pixie. Hans didn't want to leave the magical realm, but he knew that he had been entrusted with a very important responsibility. If he didn't get back to light the fire soon, it would go out and the new year would not arrive. Hans crept under the hem of January's cloak, back into the real world.

When she saw Hans, Sister December passed the staff to Brother January, who took the twelfth-night candle and re-ignited the dying fire. It leapt to life, blazing so brightly that Hans had to turn away. When he looked back a moment later, the twelve months and their fire had disappeared without a trace.

The moon had now risen, casting a pale, ethereal glow over the forest. Hans found his bearings and plodded on until he had arrived at the familiar wooden fence that surrounded his grandparents' small dwelling. No sooner had he knocked than the door flew open.

"Hans!" said his grandparents, sweeping him into their arms. "We were so worried. What happened?"

"Happy New Year," said Hans before collapsing into a chair by the hearth. His granny brought him a bowl of steaming soup but little Hans's eyes were already drooping.

"There is a Christmas cake for you in my bag, but I don't have the twelfth-night candle any more. December asked me to fetch fire to bring in the new year, so I used the candle, but now it is gone."

"Shh, there now, you're safe and warm," clucked Granny, thinking Hans's mind was addled from cold.

Hans took a few sips of soup before falling deeply asleep, dreaming happily of fairy feasts and the months of the year.

FINDING FIRE

A story from the Democratic Republic of the Congo

Long, long ago, people lived in a world without fire. The nights were so very dark and so very cold. The people huddled together to sleep, wrapped in animal skins. With no fire, there was no light to see by, so they were afraid that hungry lions would eat them while they slept. The people couldn't even cook their food – everything was raw!

It is said that ignorance is bliss, but unfortunately the people knew what fire was despite not having it for themselves. Sometimes, the lightning storms were so powerful that trees in the forest were set alight. The people were afraid of the flames, but their light, heat and power were bewitching.

The people began to dream about fire and to desire it more than anything else. Two elders, Grandmother and Grandfather, decided to call upon the animals for help. But at the meeting the animals laughed at them.

"We don't need fire," said the head of the elephants. "Your skin is too thin. That's why you get cold. You need a nice thick layer of grey skin like us elephants – it will keep you warm at night."

"What you humans need is night vision, like us," hissed the head of the snakes. "Then, you wouldn't be afraid of lions."

"Why can't you be happy with raw food? We monkeys get by just fine on fruit and leaves.

You humans are never content!" said the head of the monkeys.

That was the last straw...

"We cannot grow a new skin. We cannot develop night vision, and we don't want to eat only fruit and leaves! What we need is fire," exclaimed Grandmother.

Most of the big animals left the meeting after this outburst, thinking to themselves how silly humans were. Not all of the animals felt the same way though... Little Spider crawled over to Grandmother and Grandfather.

"I would like to help you if I can. Do you know where the fire lives?"

"In the sky," answered Grandfather.

Spider set off immediately. She scurried up the nearest tree and began to spin a thread of silk. As the silk grew in length, Spider addressed the wind.

"Wind, please will you carry me up to the bright blue sky?"

At once, the wind answered with a mighty gust that sent Spider sailing up, up, higher and higher, through the wispy clouds to the top of the bright blue sky. Once there, Spider tried to make a hole, but her little legs were not strong enough. Undeterred, she attached her silk and scuttled back down the thread again, all the way to the tree where the other end of her silk was securely tethered.

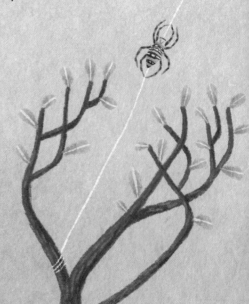

Who could Spider call on to make a hole in the sky? Of course – it had to be Woodpecker! Spider called out for Woodpecker, and he arrived right away.

"Follow me, Woodpecker. I have need of your strong beak!"

Spider climbed back up her silken thread, leading Woodpecker,

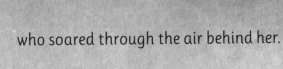

who soared through the air behind her.

When they reached the top of the sky,
Woodpecker began to tap his sturdy beak.
PECK-PECK-PECK and then suddenly,
WHOOSH! A flood of light shone through the hole.
Woodpecker kept tapping his beak until there were
lots of holes that made chinks of light in the sky.
The first stars had been revealed.

Spider congratulated Woodpecker and peered through
the holes. She saw the fire burning in the stars and called
out to it.
"Fire, the people have need of you. Will you come down to
Earth and share your light and power?"
"Is there any person brave enough to come and take me?" asked
Fire. "I will come down willingly, but only if a human carries me."

When Spider delivered this message back on Earth, the people were
agitated and avoided looking at each other. Nobody wanted to risk
their life climbing a silken thread to the top of the sky. And not only
that, but capture fire and carry it back down again? The plan was
sheer folly.
But then a strong, bold voice called out, "I will go!"

A young woman named Diba stepped forwards. The people looked
sceptical, but Diba was determined. She fetched a clay jar and a
branch, fastened them around her waist and began to climb the silk
thread. Spider went with her, cheering her on. At points, Diba became
so tired that she feared she would lose her grip and fall back to Earth.
But Spider stepped in and spun a thread to allow her to hang and rest
a while. Higher and higher Diba climbed. Daylight was fading and
darkness was falling when she at last reached the top of the sky.

38

The fire in the stars was burning
brightly and though Diba was a
little afraid, she grasped her branch
and reached up through one of the holes
in the sky. The branch caught fire at once,
and Diba placed it in her jar, then began
the long climb down. The creeping shadow
of darkness had spread its wings, but the
starlight shone her way home.

There were great celebrations when Diba arrived with
the burning branch in her jar. The people had laid up
a huge bonfire in readiness for her and cheered as she
plunged her burning branch into its heart. The flames
caught and began to leap and dance merrily. The people
rejoiced. They now had warmth, light and power thanks
to the ingenuity of a spider, the strength of a woodpecker
and the bravery of a young woman.

THE SKY GARDEN
A Gamilaraay story from Australia

Long, long ago was the Dreamtime. This was when Great Baiame created the world. Baiame made mighty mountains, rushing rivers, open oceans and fertile forests. He created life to populate these habitats – communities of humans and animals with stripes, spots, scales, fur and feathers. The last thing Baiame did was make the world beautiful. He scattered flowers everywhere so that the Earth shone with every colour imaginable. Once Baiame's work was done, he returned to his home in the sky.

For a while, the people on Earth were happy and content. They had enough to eat, and they lived in wonderful surroundings. But when Baiame stopped watching over his creation, the magic faded, and the Earth dried up. The flowers couldn't survive for long on barren soil; slowly they all began to wither and die. The colours and fragrances of Earth disappeared with the flowers, leaving it a bleak, grey place. Without flowers, the bees could not survive. And without the bees to pollinate them, many other plant species disappeared. It wasn't long before the stores of honey ran out and crops began to fail. The people of Earth became desperate. Something had to be done.

A group of wise elders came together and held a special ceremony. They danced and chanted, they drew symbols in the ground, and they waited for a sign. When the signal came at last, it was loud and clear. The elders set off immediately for Oobi-Oobi Mountain. Now, this was not just any old mountain. Its peak was the gateway to the sky, and no humans had ever dared to climb it before. It was treacherous and steeped in magic.

   When the elders reached the foot of Oobi-Oobi, they stopped short. A wall of sheer rock towered over them. There was no path. Some of the elders attempted to climb but to no avail. This was a magic

mountain, and there was no way that they could tackle
it without help.

Calmly, the elders chanted and sung, drew symbols
in the ground and waited for a sign.

After some time, their prayers were answered and a
steep path appeared in the rock face. The elders began
to climb at once, but even on the path it was terribly
hard going. Every step was a loose foothold. They were
forced to crawl, gingerly feeling their way, knowing
that one wrong move would take them tumbling
back down to Earth.

For four days and four nights they journeyed in
this way, but not once was there a suggestion of
giving up. On the fourth day, they ascended into the
misty clouds. It seemed that they would never find their
way out, but at last they dipped above the swirling fog.
They had reached the peak of the mountain and
the gateway to the sky! But to their disappointment,
there was nothing there but a bubbling stream
and a stone circle.

Once again, the elders waited patiently for a sign.
Soon enough, a gale-force wind began to blow,
carrying a voice that boomed like thunder.

"I am Walla-Guroon-Bu-An, messenger to
the Great Baiame. What are you doing here,
Earth Children? Who gave you the right
to climb this sacred mountain, and
what do you want of us?"

For the first time, the elders were
afraid. They bowed their heads
and cowered back as the
wisest among them
stepped forwards.

"Forgive us, Walla-Guroon-Bu-An. Our request is simple. When Great Baiame left the Earth, all of the flowers withered and died. This has filled the hearts of our people with such sadness. Will you help us, please?"

The elders felt themselves lifted, spinning into a twister of wind. The whirlwind transported them up to the realm of the gods and tossed them down into a soft meadow. They sat up dizzily. As their surroundings came into focus, they gasped with joy. Even in the beginning they had never seen anything like this. It was a land of flowers! Blazing, bursting blooms of every colour under the sun, growing as far as they could see. The scents that rose up were overwhelmingly delicious.

"You are in Baiame's garden now," boomed the voice of the messenger. "You may pick anything you like to take back to Earth, but hurry, Baiame will not let you linger for long."

In a frenzy, the elders began to pick everything in sight, gathering great armfuls of blooms. Before long, they began to feel the wind start up again. To their horror, the flowers they had picked turned to dust before their eyes – the colourful plumes whipped up into the air.

The whirlwind blew with a mighty force and the elders found themselves back at the base of Oobi-Oobi. Dazed, they stood up. The colourful dust flew around their heads, and the elders gave in to despair at last. All of their beautiful flowers were gone. The gods had used them as mere playthings for their own entertainment.

But what was this? The elders rubbed their eyes in disbelief. The whirling dust was taking shape – flowers began to rain down upon them! Everything that they had picked and more! The elders joined hands and danced for joy as the voice of Walla-Guroon-Bu-An echoed out.

"Be careful with these flowers. You must scatter their seeds over all the lands, and when they die, more will grow in their place. This time, Baiame will not forget to send sun and rain to make these flowers grow and flourish. At certain times of the year, the flowers will fade, just as the moon pales with the rising sun, but fear not, for they will grow again and be just as bright as the moon after sundown."

The elders returned home with their bounty and instructed the people with the words of the messenger. Seeds were scattered at every corner of the Earth, and flowers sprung up once again in the woods and valleys, the mountains and plains. With the return of the flowers, the bees came back too.

It was just as Walla-Guroon-Bu-An had said. The flowers faded every year in the autumn but they never died. Great Baiame kept his promise to water and shine light on the Earth. When the drought came again, it seemed as though the plants would never recover. But in the end there was rain, and the flowers flourished anew, just like the moon after sundown. This is the way it has always been, ever since those wise elders brought the flowers from the Sky Garden all those years ago.

43

THE DISCONTENTED PINE TREE
A story from Denmark

There was once a large forest filled with trees of all kinds. Some with short, stocky trunks, some with long, leggy limbs and a whole host of different leaves in many colours and shapes.

In amongst them was a little pine tree. She looked down at herself and sighed. *My pine needles are so dull. Nobody would ever notice me in this forest. If only I had something other than needles on my branches.*

As she was moaning and groaning, a grand carriage pulled by four smart horses rolled past. It was made from dark wood and had gold edging that glowed and glinted in the sunlight. The seats were covered in plush red velvet, and the pine tree noticed how beautifully dressed the people inside the carriage were. This made her feel even more self-conscious. *Oh, how I wish I could have needles made of gold that would glow and glint in the sunlight,* she thought.

All of the rest of that day, the poor little tree could think of nothing else. She wished and she wished and she wished.

Well, what do you know? It just so happened that the fairy folk came out that day at twilight. They drank sweet nectar out of acorn cups, chased each other over toadstools, danced in fairy rings and flew about joyfully under the trees. One of the fairies caught the pine tree's wish on the air and felt sorry for her. She blew a handful of her magic dust towards the little tree and smiled to herself.

The next morning, the pine tree's shiny green needles had disappeared. They had been replaced with solid gold needles! The little tree couldn't believe her eyes. *Oh my, oh my, just look at how beautiful I am!* she thought happily. *I'm the talk of the forest! Nobody will miss me amongst the other trees now.* She felt puffed up with pride as her needles glowed and glinted in the sun. At that moment, a pedlar was making his way through the forest, pushing his cart and muttering to

45

himself. *Can't even afford to fix this rotten wheel that's coming loose,* he grumbled.

As the pedlar turned the corner of the path, he was forced to shade his eyes. He was about to curse the sun when he realised that he had been blinded by a golden tree! The pedlar gaped in awe, and then began to rub his hands together gleefully.

The tree saw the pedlar coming and prepared to be admired. The pedlar approached her and began to run his hands over her branches. The next thing she knew, he was pulling out her needles!

"Stop! Stop!" the tree cried, but the pedlar either couldn't hear or didn't want to listen. He tugged out her needles and placed them in his cart until there were none left. Then, off he skipped with his treasure, leaving the poor pine tree with her naked branches.

What a silly tree I am, she thought. *Of course, gold was much too valuable for my needles. I should have known that, but I can't stay like this.* Suddenly, she had a thought. *Glass! It is not nearly so valuable as gold, and yet it will still look very beautiful. I will be the envy of all the other trees in the wood. Yes, glass needles are exactly what I need.*

So, she wished and she wished and she wished. And who do you think was listening? The little fairy had come back to admire her handiwork and, dismayed to see the pine tree standing bare, once again she blew her magic dust.

The next day, the tree was covered in glittering needles of glass! The gold had glinted, but the glass needles blazed like diamonds and cast little rainbows all around. The pine tree was very pleased with herself indeed. Until... a drop of rain fell. Soon enough, the wind began to howl, thunder clapped, and lightning flashed. Rain began pelting down and the wind whipped through the forest, tearing at the branches of all the trees. The glass needles were so delicate that they smashed to pieces within minutes.

When the wind died at last and the tree was able to survey the damage, she cried in despair. Her branches were bare again. All around her were scattered shards of glass, twinkling in the grass.

The tree looked around sadly, feeling ashamed. It was then that she noticed the maple tree nearby. The maple had survived the storm without a scratch. All of its leaves and branches were intact. And what leaves! They were beautiful – star shaped and a deep orange colour that stood out against the uniform green of the forest. *Maple*, thought the tree. *Why didn't I wish for maple leaves instead of wasting my time on silly materials that were totally unsuited to me?* So, she wished and she wished and she wished. And who do you think heard her?

The next morning, the little pine tree was covered in maple leaves! At first, all seemed to be well. She was pleased with their fiery colour, but nobody would want to steal them, and they would survive the wildest of storms.

However, the day wore on and the sun beat down. The pine tree started to feel that she was wilting and drying out. She was losing more moisture through her leaves than she could possibly take in from her roots. Her beautiful red leaves started to droop and the little tree felt herself becoming weaker and weaker. In desperation, she pulled all of the leaves off her branches, leaving them as bare as winter.

Whatever will I do? thought the pine tree. *Gold needles are much too valuable, glass needles are too fragile and maple leaves dry me out.*
  She reflected long and hard, and suddenly it came to her. She had been so taken up with looks and the desire to stand out that she had not spared a thought for practicality or usefulness. She realised just how perfect her original needles had been. *No one will steal pine needles because they are only valuable to me. They are strong and flexible enough to withstand storms, and their waxy coating means that they will never dry out! Yes, pine needles are just right for me!*
  She hoped and she wished, and the next morning when she woke up, the little pine tree was covered with her dear old green needles. She sighed happily, no longer caring about standing out in the forest and attracting attention. At last, she felt content to look like a little pine tree.

· ✳ ❋ ✳ ·

Go into any forest or woodland and find a pine tree. Sit quietly at its base, listen carefully, and if you are lucky, you will hear this story whispered from its branches.

THE CORN GIRL

An Iroquois story from North America

I n the beginning, the people of Earth were nomadic. This means that they never settled in one place for too long. They didn't farm the land as we do now. Instead, they foraged for a while in one place and moved on when the food ran out.

One tribe in particular had fallen on hard times and was struggling to find enough to eat. A wise old woman summoned everybody together.
"My people, I must share something that has been happening to me for the last ten nights. A sweet, haunting melody roused me from my wigwam and led me down to the shores of the lake. I have a feeling that something very good is going to come of this. Who will join me tonight in listening to this song? We must work out what it means."
 The whole village agreed to go with her as they were all amazed at her story and eager to hear this singing for themselves. That night, they stood quietly on the shore and looked out across the great lake rippling in the moonlight. Soon, some of them heard a soft melody floating across the water. It was hauntingly beautiful.

> *My ears are golden,*
> *I wave and sway.*
> *As the sun smiles,*
> *I grow each day.*

The villagers strained their eyes, searching the lake for any sign of life, but none could be found. When the old woman replied with a song of peace and welcome, the others joined in, trusting the Great Spirit who watched over them.
 The strange melody now seemed to be echoing from all sides of the lake. There was something eerie about a song without a singer, and a few of the children began to cry.
 "Go home, all of you, and leave me here," said the old woman.

"I am not afraid. I shall wait and find out who this singer is and what they want from us."

As the rest of the village departed, the old woman sat down. She didn't have long to wait before the voice came back to her. This time, it spoke rather than sang.

"Please come and bring me ashore."

At once, the old woman went to collect her canoe and paddled towards the centre of the lake. She could see a great hump ahead of her, and it was only as she got closer that she realised that the hump was an enormous beaver! On top of the beaver sat a girl with long plaits. She was graceful and elegant, and the moon's radiance seemed to shine out from her. The old woman drew her canoe alongside, and the girl leapt lightly into it. When they reached the shore, the girl told the old woman to leave her and come back in the morning.

The next day, the old woman arose and went straight to the lake. There on the shore was a single ear of corn. It was growing in exactly the spot where the girl had been sitting. The old woman bent to carefully pick the corn and carried it back to her wigwam. She wasn't sure what to do with it, so she hung the corn near her fireplace and waited for further guidance. Sure enough, that night the old woman had a dream. In it, the ear of corn became the girl she had rescued.

"Please, I am wilting so close to the fire. It is much too hot for me there. Please take me outside and plant my seeds in the ground."

When the old woman awoke, she lost no time in shaking out some of the seeds and planting them next to her wigwam. A few weeks passed before she noticed some little green shoots growing.

That night, she dreamt of the girl again.

"Well done. You have nurtured me and shown me love and care, and now I have grown. For I am Corn, and I have come to solve your problems. Sow my seeds, keep me free of weeds and tend to me. Grind me to make flour, and out of flour you can bake bread. You must share me all around. I will make your people strong, and you will have food whenever you need it."

The woman planted all of the remaining seeds and tended to them with the love of a parent. Summer came and the green stalks of corn grew golden ears under the light of the sun.

As summer faded into autumn, the corn rose to double the height of the old woman. And when the first leaves began to fall, she knew that it was time for harvest. The whole village came to help her harvest the corn, and they divided the crop equally between them. The old woman showed them how to make bread and, that night, nobody went to bed hungry.

The villagers went to the lake the next day to sing their thanks to the corn girl. They were surprised when the reply came and it was full of sadness:

Do not tak

Take care of our fragile planet;
Protect all forms of life.
Oh, the pain of waste and poison!
Do not treat me with contempt.
Do not take the Earth for granted,
Or you may lose everything.

The villagers looked at each other. What could this mean? Only the old woman understood. She bowed her head in shame because she had the gift of second sight and was able to see the path of destruction that lay ahead.

 "The Earth is sacred and so are all of the things that grow upon it. We know this, and we respect the web of life. But there will come a time when your children's children will forget this wisdom. When this happens, sorrow and hunger will reign. And the reign will never end until their grandchildren understand the only lesson that matters – respect and protect the Earth."

53

the Earth for granted, or you may lose everything.

STAIRWAY TO THE STARS
A story from England

Once upon a time, there was a little girl called Flora whose greatest wish was to touch the stars in the sky. She was mesmerised by the twinkling lights scattered in the heavens and spent night after night gazing out from her window in the tiny cottage where she lived.

One evening, as she stood stargazing with her chin in her hands, Flora decided that she had had enough of waiting around. It was time to reach for the stars.

  Flora hadn't travelled far before she came upon a millpond. Reflected on the glassy surface were glittering pinpricks of light.

  "Excuse me," said Flora to the pond, "I'm looking for the stars. Do you know where they are?"

54

"Well, just take a look! They are right here on top of me. Why not jump in and see if you can grasp one?" answered the millpond.

Flora leapt into the pond and swam around. She dove down and clutched at the silty ground, but no stars were there. She glided along the surface of the pond, scooping at the dots of light, but her hands touched only water.

Undeterred, Flora pulled herself out of the pond and walked dripping wet into the woods. Before long, she began to hear the tinkling of a brook. Eagerly, Flora trotted over to it.

"Hello, I'm on a quest to find the stars. Do you know where I might discover them?"

"Oh, yes," replied the brook. "The stars are constantly dipping in and out of my waters. Hop in, and you are bound to find a whole handful."

So, wet as she was already, Flora stepped into the brook and bent down to examine the flowing water. She searched and searched but could not find any stars. Sighing, Flora left the brook behind.

She climbed a stile and began to roam through a meadow full of

swaying, sweetly scented grass. She skipped along until she noticed a glowing area in the far corner. As she got closer, Flora saw that the luminous light came from a ring of fairies dancing merrily in a circle.

"Good evening, fairies. I wonder if you could tell me where I might find the stars?"

"Why, the stars are gleaming upon the grass. Come and join our circle, and you will see."

Flora joined hands with the fairy folk and danced until she was breathless, all the time looking hopefully for the stars. But none did she find. The gleaming studs of light on the grass were merely drops of dew. Flora sat down crossly.

"I'll never touch the stars. I've looked here, there and everywhere, and they will not be found!"

The fairy folk took pity on Flora.

"Now, look. If you really want to find the stars you must look up, not down. Leave the meadow and keep going until you find Four-Feet. Ask the creature to take you to No-Feet. No-Feet will carry you to the staircase without steps. If you can climb the staircase, then you may find what you are looking for."

Flora hurried off across the meadow and out onto a dirt track. It wasn't long before she came upon a beautiful dappled mare standing beneath a rowan tree. The horse was the colour of honey, and it whickered softly when it saw her. *Four feet,* Flora thought to herself. *This must be the creature.*

"Will you take me to No-Feet so that I may find the stars?" asked Flora.

Four-Feet gently inclined her head and knelt down so that Flora could climb onto her broad back. The horse raced over the countryside as gracefully as a hare. Before Flora knew it, they had arrived at a wide expanse of sea. On the horizon was a dazzling belt of colours that arched up from the water and disappeared into the dark sky.

"Here the land meets the sea. This is as far as I can take you."

In a moment, Four-Feet was gone and Flora was left alone. Or was she? Approaching the water, Flora noticed a pale silver shape beneath the waves. *Aha! No feet!*

Flora crouched next to the water and trailed her fingers through it. At once, the fish raised its head.

"I am on a journey to find the stars. Please, if you are No-Feet, will you take me to the stairs without steps?"

A moment later, Flora was on the fish's back and they were ploughing through the waves. They soon reached the belt of colours.

"Well, here you are. This is the staircase without steps. But do beware – these stairs are not easy to scale. It will be a long and arduous journey. Are you sure you can manage?"

"I've come this far, and I'm not giving up now," said Flora stubbornly, stifling a yawn.

She began to climb, but it wasn't so much climbing as treading air... Flora didn't feel as though she were moving at all. When she reached up to hold on to the belt of light, her hand went straight through it. It was like wading through treacle, and Flora soon started to feel that it was a hopeless mission. But then she looked down and realised with delight that the sea was now twinkling far, far below her. Encouraged, she started climbing again with new enthusiasm.

Time passed and Flora began to shiver. The air was colder, sharper and crisper – her breath escaped in smoky plumes. Flora turned to look up and gasped in wonder. She had reached the end of the staircase!

The stars had always looked beautiful from the Earth, but up here they were magnificent. Each star shone and glittered with all the colours of the rainbow.

On Earth, you might have been lucky enough to glimpse the odd shooting star, but up here Flora could barely follow all the movement. It was as though the stars were chasing each other across the sky, casting trails like powdered sherbet.

The stars seemed so close now – surely she could just reach out a hand... A star came whizzing towards her and Flora lunged towards it but, as she did, she lost her footing on the staircase.

57

Flora was falling, falling back towards the Earth, but she wasn't frightened. As she drifted down, Flora had the irresistible feeling that one gets just before falling asleep.

When she opened her eyes, she was back in the little cottage, in her own soft bed. Sunlight streamed through the open window, and she could hear the happy, familiar sounds of her mother lighting the fire and preparing breakfast. *I did it!* thought Flora to herself. *I found the stars in the sky and I touched one. I really did.*

But even as she thought this, doubts began to creep into her mind. Everything seemed so normal and ordinary now. She started to feel sorrowful, thinking that it must have been a dream after all.

Flora sat up and opened her clenched fist to rub her eye. Well, what do you think she found in the palm of her hand? A dazzling speck of stardust glinting gently with all the colours of the rainbow.

THE DEER'S ANTLERS
A story from Greece

T he forest was in the first bloom of spring. Snowdrops were poking their heads through the soil, and tight little buds were beginning to unfurl. The sun was ripening the world that had been under winter's blanket for so long.

Deer was feeling very pleased. It was a relief to him when spring arrived and new grasses and shoots began to appear. His antlers were fully grown, and he felt puffed up with pride. Happily, he trotted towards a pool of water for a drink. It was a still day, and the surface of the pool was smooth and glassy.

As Deer bent his head to take a drink, he caught sight of himself in the pool's mirror. His antlers shone in the sunlight. *Just look at those handsome antlers,* he thought to himself. *I should be king of the forest with such a crown as this!* He inclined his head further to reach the water and his gaze fell to his legs. *Oh dear,* he thought. *What terribly spindly legs I have. I'll never be king of the forest with such bandy, skinny legs.*

Deer felt ashamed. Where a moment before he had been strutting through the woodland, Deer now shrank back beneath the trees with head and antlers bowed. All of a sudden, he caught the whiff of something that made him freeze: the unmistakable smell of a wolf.

A twig snapped close by and Deer leapt forwards. He bounded through the forest as fast as he could until he came upon a prickly thicket obscuring the way. Next to the thicket was a large oak tree with low-hanging branches. Beyond it, Deer could see a meadow. If he could just get to the meadow, then he knew he could outrun the wolf easily. But hard as he tried, Deer couldn't fit underneath the oak's branches.

He could now hear the panting of the wolf coming up behind him...

Deer gave a desperate push and managed to use his antlers to break through. On long, nimble legs, he jumped over the bank and out into the meadow to safety. The wolf was left far behind.

The next time that Deer went for a drink, he noted his reflection once again. He looked at his crown of antlers. *Not only beautiful but useful for breaking through tight spaces.* His gaze dropped down to his legs. *Look at these! Legs that can run, leap, bound and carry me away from predators who wish to do me harm! How lucky I am!*

And with that, Deer was off, dancing and prancing through the forest, at last proud of who he was.

THE FIRST WOODPECKER
A story from Romania

Katrina lived a simple life in a small village in rural Romania. The people of the village tended to stay put, never venturing too far afield. This meant that everybody knew the business of everyone else. Anything out of the ordinary was received with great excitement, because it presented the opportunity to herald the village with news.

This may explain why Katrina was quite so interested in the old man whom she met when out walking one day. Visitors didn't come to their remote village all that often, and he was dressed very oddly in a long cloak and a pointed, wide-brimmed hat. Katrina approached him at once.

"Good day, Sir. What business brings you to our village?"

The old man eyed her shrewdly.

"I am lost, Sister. I'm looking for the sea. Is it very far?"

"No, not very," answered Katrina.

"Ah, good. Well, my dear, I wonder whether you might do me a favour."

"That depends on the favour," said Katrina, who was no fool.

The man smiled.

"What if I told you that you would be rewarded handsomely for your part? The task is simple. Take this bag to the sea and throw it in. You shall have a sack of gold in return."

Katrina couldn't believe her luck. Not only would she have a marvellous story to tell everyone but this old crackpot would pay her for it! She held her hands out for the bag.

"There is one condition... You must not look inside the bag under any circumstance," warned the old man.

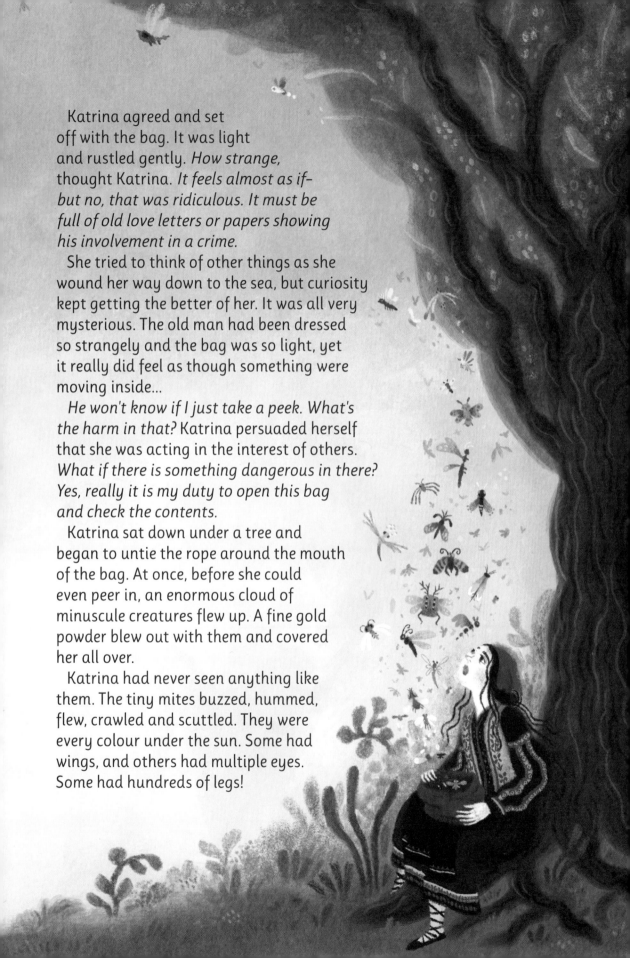

Katrina agreed and set
off with the bag. It was light
and rustled gently. *How strange,*
thought Katrina. *It feels almost as if–*
but no, that was ridiculous. It must be
full of old love letters or papers showing
his involvement in a crime.

She tried to think of other things as she
wound her way down to the sea, but curiosity
kept getting the better of her. It was all very
mysterious. The old man had been dressed
so strangely and the bag was so light, yet
it really did feel as though something were
moving inside...

He won't know if I just take a peek. What's
the harm in that? Katrina persuaded herself
that she was acting in the interest of others.
What if there is something dangerous in there?
Yes, really it is my duty to open this bag
and check the contents.

Katrina sat down under a tree and
began to untie the rope around the mouth
of the bag. At once, before she could
even peer in, an enormous cloud of
minuscule creatures flew up. A fine gold
powder blew out with them and covered
her all over.

Katrina had never seen anything like
them. The tiny mites buzzed, hummed,
flew, crawled and scuttled. They were
every colour under the sun. Some had
wings, and others had multiple eyes.
Some had hundreds of legs!

Katrina tried her best to catch them, but they were much too fast for her. More kept spilling out every time she opened the bag to put one back. It was no good – the tide of creatures was unstoppable, and Katrina couldn't even hold the bag shut. Not knowing what else to do, she ran after the fluttering trail of mites. They were all heading for the forest.

As Katrina ran, something extraordinary started to happen. She felt herself shrinking! The features of her face sharpened into a pointed beak, and feathers started to sprout from her skin. The feathers were black, the same colour her dress had been. A little tuft of red feathers took the place of the red scarf that had been tied around her head. Wings burst from her shoulder blades and her feet became claws.

The strange man was a sorcerer, and his bag had been filled with magic. When Katrina let it escape, she introduced the first insects to the world, and the golden dust turned her into the world's first woodpecker!

To this day, if you see a woodpecker, you will notice that it is constantly searching and pecking into any cracks or crevices it can find. This is because woodpeckers are still trying to collect all of the insects and put them back into the magician's bag.

DAY WITHOUT NIGHT
A story from India

In the beginning, when the world was new, the Earth spun beneath the constant glare of the sun. Darkness was unimaginable. Earth's people knew only of daylight accompanied by endless work and toil. For in these early times there was much work to do, and the word 'rest' was meaningless. Rest? When there were fields to dig, seeds to plant, animals to tend, huts to build, water to fetch...

The people of Earth worked like busy termites, hurrying hither and thither. As soon as one job was completed, it was on to the next. Children worked just as hard! There was no time for play, learning or idleness. Life meant work, and that was all.

One day, the creator decided to take a stroll around the Earth. He smiled when he saw the neat fields and terraces; the abundance of fruit and vegetables; the peaceful, contented animals; and the tidy huts. *What an excellent job I have done*, thought the creator smugly. *What good thinking it was to make it never-ending day. These lucky people can enjoy the sunshine and will never know the darkness.*

The creator approached a young man who was furiously digging.

"Well, my son. Are you happy here on Earth?"

"Happy?" the man said, puzzled. "I don't know what that means. I work, and that is all."

The creator frowned. "Yes, you all work very hard, but what about rest? Do you enjoy playing games or talking with neighbours under the shade of the tree?"

"Rest?" asked the man. "I'm sorry, but I don't follow your meaning. I work, and that is all."

What a strange man, thought the creator. He moved on to a woman nursing her baby.

"Hello, my child. What a beautiful baby. When was she born?"

"Today," said the woman.

The creator was confused – the baby looked at least six months old.

Moving on, he approached an old man repairing the roof of his hut.

"Old man, when did you begin these repairs?" asked the creator.

"Today," answered the man.

"And when did you build this fine hut?"

"Today."

"And that wonderful old tree over there. When was it planted?"

"Why, today of course. When else?" asked the old man with confusion.

At last, the creator understood: the sun never set, so the people had no understanding of time. To the people of Earth, 'today' meant past, present and future. The creator travelled back to the heavens.

"Sun – you must stop constantly shining. The people are confused and have no idea of time. From now on, you must shine during the day and start to set towards evening. Allow darkness to reign through the night, and then rise again in the morning. People will not be able to work in the darkness and will learn to rest."

Sun agreed, and the next evening sank down below the horizon. Before long, Earth was steeped in darkness. The people were terrified. They had never known anything except daylight and thought that the world was ending! One of the elders commanded the people to lie down to protect themselves. At once, they felt their bodies sigh with pleasure as they fell into the first deep sleep of their lives.

In the morning, the sun rose again and the people blinked awake sleepily to begin their work as normal.

After a few days, they realised that the world would not end when the sun set. The creator travelled back to Earth to check on them.

"Do you feel happier now that you have time for rest as well as work?"

"We certainly feel better and have fewer aches and pains. There is one thing though... When the sun goes down, it is so dark that we become completely blind. We are always breaking things and bumping into each other or falling over," said one of the elders.

The creator returned to the heavens to think the problem over. *If I ask Sun to shine in the night, the people will start to work again. But why not make a companion for Sun? A celestial body of soft and gentle light, just enough to see by, but not too strong to sleep through.* With a flourish, the glowing moon was born!

The people learnt to relax. Children were allowed to play and learn instead of being put to work as soon as they could walk. Adults chatted and sang while they worked and took the time to sit and eat together. Stories had not existed before, but now they flowed from the mouths of people who had time to use their imaginations and drink in what they saw around them. At last the true meanings of work, rest and happiness were understood.

KING AND QUEEN OF THE SKIES
A story from Nigeria

Abassi was the man in the moon and the King of the Skies. He was married to Atai, the brightest and most brilliant of all the stars. One day, they had a quarrel that was to have terrible consequences...

The stars, who were Atai's subjects, thought that she deserved to be the Queen of the Skies. Stars were used for navigation by sailors, and wise people could look to the heavens to read their fortunes and make predictions about the future. The stars decided that they and their queen were more useful than Abassi. After all, his only talents were setting, rising and shining. Atai quite agreed! But Abassi was very proud, and when he began to hear these rumours, he became furious.

I was around long before people started to sail or study astrology, he thought angrily. He decided to punish the stars and put them in their place. He wanted to prevent them from shining but he couldn't extinguish their light without help, so he sought out thunder, lightning, wind and rain.

"The stars have become very arrogant," he told them. "They have been going around saying that they are better than all of us! We must teach them a lesson."

This wasn't strictly true, but Abassi needed the support of the elements. Before long, he had managed to whip them into a fury. The rain lashed down, the wind howled and raged, thunder boomed and lightning seared through the sky. Earth had never known a storm like it. Forests, deserts and villages were destroyed. Humans and animals were forced to retreat to caves and mountaintops. The Earth was shrouded in darkness; no light was able to get through the thick walls of cloud. No sun, no moon and no stars.

Abassi had successfully stopped the stars from shining, but now he could not cast any light either. However, he didn't care. His only concern was to cause suffering to Atai and the stars.

69

Meanwhile, the elements were revelling in their new-found power, and the storm showed no sign of abating. Earth was in a terrible state. The land had been swallowed up by ocean and only the very tops of the mountains were safe. The people and animals had been plunged into darkness for weeks on end and things were desperate. The people were struggling to stave off the wild animals who wanted to eat them!

The little stars felt sorry for the Earth. They knew that they had played a part in this terrible stalemate, and they missed being able to shine. The stars begged Atai to let them speak to Abassi. If they didn't act soon, Earth would be destroyed. Atai was proud but not stupid. Grudgingly, she agreed.

When the stars arrived to speak to Abassi, they found themselves more welcome than they would have guessed. He himself was none too happy about the situation. Not only had he lost his wife, but he had also given up his role as King of the Skies. So, Atai and Abassi agreed to patch things up, but this was not the end of the story...

The elements liked being in control of the skies and were not willing to give this honour up in a hurry. After much discussion, the following agreement was settled on: when the moon was shining his brightest, the stars would fade out, allowing him full majesty as King of the Skies. But when the moon started to set, the stars would have the chance to shine as brightly as they liked. Then, Atai would rise up and take over as Queen of the Skies, bathing the world in light.

Lastly, there would be certain times when the elements were allowed full control. During these periods, Abassi, Atai and all of the stars would have to extinguish themselves and allow for stormy darkness.

To this day, there is still no agreement about who has the greater majesty. Some are awed by the full moon on his placid journey through the night sky, while others prefer the brilliance of the sun and her stars. Some feel the greatest honour should go to the elements with their noisy performances of power and dominion.

What do you think?

THE FLOWER THIEF
A story from Syria

The palace gardens of King Adil and Queen Zaida were the finest in Arabia. Stretching for miles, they boasted a vast array of flowers, plants, orchards and groves, and were a sanctuary for many wild creatures.

Closest to the palace was the flower garden. This was where the king and queen spent most of their time. They were keen botanists and had collected thousands of different plants and flowers from all over the world. Whenever visitors from far realms came to stay, they would bring a new seed. The flower garden had been divided up to represent the four corners of the Earth. Each new seed would be ceremoniously planted according to the area it belonged to. King Adil and Queen Zaida's garden enabled them to travel the world every day.

The flower garden was a delight in the summer. As soon as the buds began to unfurl, hosts of birds and insects were drawn in. Beautiful scents wafted through the air, and the many-coloured blooms created a rich palette. It really was a feast for the eyes!

The king and queen were particularly proud of their rare flower collection, which they had built up over many years. Some of these blooms were one of a kind.

One morning, on their walk through the rare flower collection, the king gasped.

"What is it, dear?" asked Queen Zaida.

"Someone has stolen our rarest flower!" exclaimed the king indignantly. "Just look! The stem is broken and one crushed petal lies next to it."

He picked it up and cradled it sadly. The garden was patrolled by guards during the day, so the thief, whoever it was, must have come by cover of night...

The king and queen had three sons, and they asked Nabil, their eldest, to sleep outside and keep watch. The trouble was that they prepared a bed for Nabil so that he would be comfortable.

Well, Nabil got a little too comfortable. He was woken the next morning by bright sunshine. Cursing, he leapt to his feet and went to inspect the rare flowers. Another bloom had been plucked. Tail between his legs, the prince went to report back to his angry father and mother.

The next night, the king and queen asked Farid, their middle child, to keep watch. Not wanting to make the same mistake, they merely laid a mat and cushions on the grass for him. Despite their precautions, Farid also fell into a deep slumber and woke to find that yet another precious bloom had been stolen.

Karam, the third and youngest son, was summoned. He was given no bed or mat, and was told that he must sit on the cold ground and on no account fall asleep!

Karam was eager to please, and in order to stop himself from dozing off, he took a bucket of icy water outside with him. Every time he felt his eyes begin to droop, the prince dunked his head into the bucket to shock his body back into wakefulness.

It was late and the moon had risen, casting a pale glow over the gardens. Karam lowered his head into the bucket for the umpteenth time when, all of a sudden, he felt the ground shake beneath him. An awful sight appeared, and the prince shrank back in horror.

It was an *ifrit*, one of the terrifying demons that transform out of smoke into creatures with horns, great wings and eyes that blaze red with fire.

The *ifrit* marched over to the rare flowers and crouched down to pick one. Karam could smell singed grass where the monster's footsteps had burnt into the ground.

Just as the demon was about to take a flower, Karam lunged forwards and tried to drive his sword into its hand. It was as though he had tried to stab a cloud; the sword met no resistance at all.

Despite the failed attack, the creature had clearly been spooked. Leaving the flowers, it turned and charged back the way it had come.

The next morning, the three princes set off to try to find the *ifrit*. It was easy enough, they just had to follow its blackened footprints.

The princes followed the tracks right to the edge of the gardens, where they stopped at an ancient well. The three boys peered into it cautiously. There was no water inside, just a deep, dusty pit. Nabil announced that he would be the first to look for the *ifrit*.

The others lowered him into the well by a rope. He was only a few feet down, however, when he shrieked, "Let me up! Let me up right now! The *ifrit* is after me!"

When Farid and Karam had hauled him up, it became apparent that the terrifying *ifrit* had been nothing more than a jumping shadow cast by Nabil's lantern.

"I'll go, then," said Farid confidently.

He made it about halfway down before he, too, began screaming to be pulled up. But it turned out that the clanging noise he had thought to be the *ifrit* was actually his sword bumping against the side of the well.

It was Karam's turn. Without fuss, he climbed into the rope harness, and his brothers inched him down into the pit.

After a long time, the taut rope became loose. Karam had reached the bottom, and there he found a tunnel. He crept along the dusty passageway, feeling his way as he went – it was pitch black and the walls of the tunnel were wet and slimy.

As he tiptoed further along, he saw a pinprick of light appear. A strange rumbling sound filled his ears and he smelt the foul tell-tale smoke of the *ifrit*. As he approached the light, Karam spied a gleaming marble chamber. He flattened himself against the wall and peered in...

The *ifrit* was asleep; the strange rumbling was the sound of its awful snoring. In the centre of the chamber was a roughly hewn stone throne, and sitting upon it was a young woman.

The *ifrit* had laid its gruesome head in her lap and she was trapped. Despite her predicament, the woman did not look afraid; instead, her expression gave off an air of strength and resolve. She sat up very straight on the throne, and Karam noticed that she was wearing a necklace made from the stolen flowers. Oddly, they had not wilted.

In fact, they looked even more luminous and precious than they had in the garden.

Karam felt his fear turn to anger. His blood boiled and he laid a hand on his sword, ready to run at the demon and slay it there and then, but the maiden had seen him. She held a hand up to stop him and beckoned him with a finger on her lips.

Karam crept over, hardly daring to breathe as he passed the *ifrit*. She whispered softly, "Do not be hasty and foolish. The demon cannot be slain by human hands. If you try to kill it, we will both die. See that rock over there?"

Karam nodded.

"Pick it up and slide it under the *ifrit*'s head while I slip from under it. Then we can both escape."

Together, they began the delicate operation of sliding the rock inch by inch under the head of the *ifrit* in order not to wake it.

At last, the demon lay on a pillow of stone. Faint with relief, the prince tried to lead the mysterious woman back the way he had come but she shook her head and gestured to a different passageway.

They soon came out into a sumptuous garden, and at last the woman stopped.

"I am Princess Amira. The *ifrit* kidnapped me while I was out picking flowers one day. The creature said that it had fallen in love with me

and that it would create the garden of my dreams in return for
my love. I've been here for five years, pretending to love the demon,
waiting for a rescue mission that I feared would never come. The *ifrit*
keeps watch over me at all times. And when it leaves to find me flowers,
it blocks all of the passages to the chamber so that I am trapped. Does
that sound like love to you?"

"No, indeed," stammered Karam, awed by this woman and her
fierce spirit.

Suddenly, a voice called out, "Who goes there?"

They both jumped as a bearded man appeared from behind an
ancient cypress tree.

"Gardener!" said Amira in recognition. "Please, help us. We escaped
the *ifrit* but there is not much time. It will soon wake and realise the
trick we played."

"Look over there," said the gardener, gesturing. "You will see a black
ram and a white ram. Only one of them can take you home. You must
decide which it is."

No sooner had the gardener uttered these words than he disappeared.
The rams were up ahead of them, racing at each other and butting
their horns.

"Shouldn't we discuss-?" Karam began but Amira was off.

"Wait!" he shouted as Amira charged straight towards the white ram and grabbed it by the horns. To his amazement, both rams immediately became still and started to nuzzle her. She climbed onto the back of the white ram, and Karam had no choice but to follow.

The next thing they knew, Amira and Karam were back in the rare flower garden. There was Karam's bucket of water and there were the broken stems.

"But how did you know which ram to choose?" asked Karam.

Amira only smiled.

Amira and Karam became best friends and, in time, were married. The stewardship of the palace gardens passed over to the couple, and they tended to them with great love and care. They continued the tradition of asking guests to bring seeds when they visited, and their four corners of the world grew even more exotic and bounteous.

Sometimes, it was hard to believe that their adventure had really happened, but the *ifrit* was not forgotten. Amira kept her necklace of flowers and wore it often. Remarkably, those petals never wilted or lost their lustre. They remained as bright and fragrant as the day they were picked, all those many years ago.

SEARCHING FOR SUMMER

A Wabanaki story from North America

Glooskap and his people lived in the Land of the Dawn. They were the people of light, and their home was blessed with great beauty. On the coastal side, a great expanse of ocean shimmered on and on. Further inland were glassy lakes hugged by craggy mountains, and forests that rippled like silk in the wind.

The people of light lived in harmony with nature and one another. They hunted, fished, gathered and grew all the food they needed, sharing what they had.

Glooskap looked after his people and treated them with great kindness. The people of light were happy and content. There was no disorder, and why should there be? Their society was just and fair.

And then, one day, the frost came. This was not unusual and did not cause any distress at first. The weather was always cold for part of the year. But months passed and instead of the thaw they all expected, a blanket of snow fell and covered the land. More cold weather followed, and the snow stayed frozen in enormous drifts.

The wigwams that the people of light lived in were made from birch bark and animal hides. They were built for mild weather, not howling, icy gales. The forlorn tents were hung with icicles, and the people huddled inside around fires, barely managing to stay warm.

The crops withered, the animals disappeared and the lakes froze over. The people of light were running low on food. The time to act had come.

Glooskap set off the very next morning. He had decided to find Winter and demand a return to their normal climate. On powerful legs, he darted across the land, travelling north.

As he journeyed further and further, the air became colder and more biting until it was painful to inhale. Glooskap's long hair had frozen solidly and thwacked against his back as he ran.

At last, he arrived at the very tip of the northland. It was so cold that water froze within seconds. Ahead of Glooskap stood an enormous wigwam. It was Winter's abode, carved entirely from ice. He entered and came face to face with Winter, who seemed to be expecting him.

"Ah, there you are, Glooskap. Come, sit down. Rest your weary legs."

"Thank you, Winter," said Glooskap with chattering teeth.

"You're not cold, are you?" asked Winter. "Here, let us talk of olden times."

Glooskap sat down and hugged his knees, trying to stop the cold that was creeping through his veins and threatening to turn his heart to ice.

As they sat together, Winter regaled Glooskap with tales of his former glory. Tales from the olden days when Winter had been almighty, holding the whole world in his icy embrace. Back then, his chilly breath had been enough to keep the Earth frozen all year round.

"And now I have frozen the land all the way down to your country, Glooskap. The people of light will become the people of ice!"

Glooskap heard this only faintly. It was the strangest thing – despite the frozen atmosphere, he was beginning to feel quite warm, and his eyes were drooping uncontrollably. *Just one quick doze before I figure out how to thwart Winter,* he thought before slipping into a sleep as deep as hibernation.

Winter had overcome the unsuspecting Glooskap with his frost charm, breathing a numbing spell over him. Glooskap slept soundly in a cocoon of ice. It was six whole months before his spirit managed to break free and he awakened, splitting open the cocoon.

Glooskap sprinted away from Winter and his wigwam of ice with a heavy heart. How could he return to the people of light and tell them that he had

failed? He looked to the skies, brushing away his frozen tears and noticed a shadow high above him.

A beautiful bird soared through the sky, elegant neck outstretched.
  "Kwee-moo!" shouted Glooskap in joyful recognition.
  It was his very own messenger, a loon – the fierce, wild bird of the lakes.
  "Where have you been, Glooskap?" asked Kwee-moo. "I've been searching for you for these six months past."
  Glooskap told Kwee-moo the whole sorry tale. When he had finished, Kwee-moo began to describe a land far to the south that was warm and temperate all year round. It was a land of plenty, a beautiful place filled with flower meadows, lush forests and rolling plains. It was ruled by Summer. Kwee-moo assured Glooskap that she was strong enough to overpower Winter.

At once, Glooskap set off for the south shores. When he reached the sea, he began to sing the song of the whales. Soon, a faithful old friend bobbed her head above the waves and blew a spume of water in greeting. This whale had carried Glooskap on all of his journeys over the sea. Glooskap leapt onto the whale's back and they were off – cruising over the deep ocean on foamy waves.

After many days of travel, Glooskap noticed a change in the air. It was no longer cold with a sharp, salty scent. Now, Glooskap felt warm currents, and he sniffed enticing hints of sweet, rich scents on the breeze. He could sense that they were close to land. Sure enough, the glittering sea soon gave way to a sandy shore.

Glooskap jumped off the whale and bade her farewell. He was enchanted by the land he found himself in. Never had he seen such an abundance of nature. He felt giddy with all the new sights and smells.

Venturing further inland, he followed the sound of music and laughter. The voices led him into a shady forest. A clearing ahead of him revealed a gathering of women in a circle. One was singing, and another kept the beat with a small drum.

The music was exquisite. In the middle of the circle danced a woman whose flowing hair was braided with flowers. She was bathed in golden sunlight, and the rays seemed to follow her every move. The woman carried blooms in her arms and, when she danced, the plants and animals nearby seemed to move and sway in time with her. This woman could be none other than Summer.

Glooskap felt compelled to join her, and the women parted to let him through. Together they danced, and Glooskap felt every care he'd ever had fall away. Winter's embrace had squeezed the life out of Glooskap, but the caress of Summer filled him with such vitality that his heart wanted to burst with love and joy.

Together, Summer and Glooskap travelled back to the far north to find Winter and stop him once and for all.

They arrived at the frozen wigwam. There, Winter rubbed his hands gleefully, ready to send Glooskap back into hibernation. But old Winter hadn't counted on Summer being there too. She hid outside the wigwam and channelled her strength into Glooskap as he began to talk.

This time, the tables were turned and Winter was forced to listen. Glooskap's own power, coupled with Summer's strength, soon sent rivulets of water down Winter's face. He was melting! The icy wigwam creaked and cracked before collapsing upon the fast-melting snow.

Summer flew all over the far north on nimble feet, casting sunshine and sweet warmth over everything until there was no snow or ice to be seen. Winter wept bitter tears to see his land taken over in this way. He was so distraught that Summer took pity on him.

"I have proved my prowess over you, Winter, and now I will relent. You may rule over the far north all year round, and you may venture into Glooskap's country for six months each year. But never again must you grip the Land of the Dawn with such force."

Grudgingly, Winter agreed, and Glooskap returned south. Summer came with him and danced over the land with her sunbeams. The hard-packed snow melted into rivers, small green shoots inched out of the soft earth and the people of light rejoiced to hear the birds sing again. Buds appeared on the trees, the animals returned and the forests rippled once more in the wind.

For half the year, Glooskap and his people made merry in the sultry weather brought by Summer. For the other half, Winter came creeping back, but he never reigned as harshly as before.

The pact made long ago continues to this day. At Winter's arrival, Summer dances away to the southland, but she always comes again six months later, ready to drive Winter back to the far north.

SOULS OF THE EARTH
A story from South Sudan

Juok, the creator, made the world and filled it with teeming rainforests, mighty mountains, wide oceans, raging rivers, grassy plains and dry deserts. Juok had populated these habitats with birds, beasts and fish. The creatures gave the world colour, noise and movement, but something was missing...
Aha! There were no people.

Juok decided to mould human beings out of the very earth that they would stand upon. The creator started in the land that would be home to the Shilluk people and ventured to the River Nile. This was the longest river in all of his creation and it supported many beautiful creatures. Crocodiles prowled the waters searching for their next meal, hippos lumbered in to take refuge from the beating sun and turtles glided contentedly on the currents.

Juok bent down to the riverbank and took a big handful of earth the colour of ebony. Lovingly, he began to mould and shape it. *I will give the people legs so that they can move about,* Juok thought. *If they have legs, they can run, walk, hop and skip.* With life-giving hands, Juok created many pairs of legs and set them down on the land, watching as they tottered along uncertainly. *Hmmm, no good. They will need arms and hands in order to work – for growing food, holding tools, building dwellings and cooking.*

The creator took another handful of earth from the riverbank and fashioned arms and hands, which he added to the bodies of the humans. The figures walked about with hands outstretched, still unable to work. *Of course!* thought Juok. *How can these poor people do a thing if they don't have eyes to see with?* He rolled balls of earth to make heads for the people and added eyeballs to their faces.

For a while, it seemed that Juok's work was done. He sat back to enjoy the sight of busy people. He was impressed by what they achieved on the first day, but by the second day it seemed that they were losing steam. The people lay down and were unable to get up. At last, it came to Juok – they had no mouths, so could not eat and give themselves energy! The humans were completely exhausted. Very gently, Juok took each person and created a mouth. Immediately, the hungry people started eating with ravenous appetites.

Again, Juok thought that his work was done and settled down. The humans were very industrious. They worked from dawn till dusk. At first, Juok was pleased with what he saw, but as time passed he began to notice the quiet. The people beavered away at their tasks in dreadful silence. The birds squawked, chirruped and sang; the beasts howled, roared and barked; but the humans were completely mute. *Tongues! My humans need tongues to speak and sing and shout. They must be able to express their feelings of anger or sadness or joy. Once they have tongues to sing, they will be able to use their arms and legs to dance and play instruments.*

Juok placed tongues in the mouths of the people and waited for the merriment to begin. To his surprise, nothing much changed. Sounds were made, but there was no new interaction between people. No singing, dancing or talking. Juok was puzzled, but then it came to him. And how obvious it seemed now... *Ears! How could the people dance and talk and make music together if they could not hear themselves or each other?*

Taking more earth from the riverbank, Juok moulded ears for the Shilluk people. With joy, he watched the change come over his little humans. At first, they were startled. Their world had been silent, and now it was bursting with all sorts of confusing sounds! Gradually, the shock and bewilderment faded to curiosity and, finally, understanding and communication. The Shilluk people discovered language and formed deep relationships with one another. They used their voices for singing and storytelling, their bodies for moving and dancing.

At last, the people could listen to the sounds of the world around them: the raging river, the whistling wind, the forest hullabaloo and the morning birdsong.

Juok was very pleased with the Shilluk people. He was now ready to travel the Earth and create more communities of humans. Juok set out to make human beings from the land of every continent. The soil of the world was varied, with different regions producing their own distinct hue. Juok moulded people with skin tones in an amazing spectrum of colours: from deep umber to burnt sienna to pale ochre and everything in between! At last, Juok sat back contentedly. He had created a wonderful world, and all of his people were beautiful.

SELKIE ISLAND

A story from Scotland

F ar, far to the north of Scotland, there lived a family of crofters, farming folk. Their little dwelling was up on the cliffs, overlooking the wide expanse of the Atlantic Sea. On a clear day, pods of orcas, bottlenose dolphins and humpback whales could be spotted in the glittering waters. Above the waves, ospreys soared – mighty sea hawks ready to snatch sleepy fish with grasping talons.

The croft was surrounded by moorland and sheltered by a line of craggy hills to the east. It was a wild, rugged landscape: bleak and wind-torn in winter but beautiful in summer when the heather was in bloom. Then, the clifftops and hillsides erupted in rosy pinks and moody purples.

The little stone house had a thatched roof of heather, and it was whitewashed so that it stood out like a gleaming star on the coastline. The farmer and his wife had five sons, and the family of seven lived together. They grew oats and barley and kept a few sheep. Now that the lads were growing into young men, it was becoming harder and harder to grow enough to feed everyone.

The old crofter had been a fisherman in his younger years. The boys all knew how to fish but until now had spent most of their time working on the croft. It was agreed that the three youngest sons – Davie, Sandy and William – would start fishing instead and see if they could make a living from the sea to help provide for the family.

The next morning, the crofter and his sons hauled the little fishing boat and nets down to the bay below their house.

"The fishing is fair by the bay, but if you really want to make a catch, you'll be better off rowing a few miles out. However, you must make sure to avoid Selkie Island," advised the crofter, gesturing towards a rocky outcrop.

Over the next few weeks, the lads managed to catch some good hauls.

They took these to the nearest market town to sell and earned some silver. But it was hard work rowing out so far and avoiding the island. The wind buffeted their boat about, and they were constantly worried about being capsized. Each day, they allowed themselves to drift a little closer to Selkie Island. The waters around there were calmer and they found an abundance of fish.

A few weeks passed before the sons began to notice that their catch was dwindling. And not only that, but they found that their nets were being chewed by something. Could there be an angry fish with teeth sharp enough to cut through their nets?

After another day of pitiful fishing and an evening spent mending the nets yet again, the old crofter overheard the boys muttering darkly to each other about sea monsters. He roared with laughter.

"What's this about sea monsters eating all the fish?" he asked.

"Well, what else could it be, Father? Something vicious in the sea is out to get us!" replied Davie, who was the youngest.

"There's no sea monster eating your nets; it's the seals!"

The lads reddened, realising their mistake, but their shame turned quickly to anger.

"Well, those seals are taking all of our catch and leaving us with the sea dregs," said Sandy, the middle brother.

"What are you talking about? Don't you realise that the seals have wee ones of their own to feed? They are not greedy creatures. They only take what they need," said their father tersely.

"Greedy or not, they are a menace and we need to do something about them," protested William, the next oldest.

The old crofter's voice dropped to a low growl.

"I told you not to fish near Selkie Island. You will leave those seals be. I have an understanding with them based on kindness and respect."

The sons scowled, but no more was said on the matter. The following day, they rowed out further than they ever had before, trying to reach beyond the seals' territory. The brothers stayed out later than usual, and it was only when the glowing sun began to dip behind the hills that they realised the time. As they sculled past Selkie Island, William called out.

"Stay the oars a minute. Look!"

A narrow mouth in the rock exposed a sandy cove where hundreds of seals lay.

"This must be the time of day that they come onto the island to rest," said Sandy.

The brothers looked at each other with the same menacing glint in their eyes. As they rowed back towards the shore, they plotted to defy their father and take matters into their own hands...

The next day, the boys went out fishing and came home as usual. They ate supper with the family and tried to act normally. After supper, their mother sat down to darn socks, while their father and older brothers strode out to check on the livestock. The younger boys took their chance. Grabbing a club each, they made their way hastily down to the shore and out to sea.

They soon arrived at the sandy cove and hauled the boat above the tideline. Then, they lay in wait. As twilight ink seeped across the sky, the boys started to get fidgety.

"Perhaps we should head on home. I have an uneasy feeling... Surely the seals should be here by now," said Davie.

"Stop your moaning," muttered William.

But Sandy took pity on little Davie.

"Here, Davie. Let's collect some driftwood and make a fire. That way, we can keep warm and maybe even tell a few tales while we wait."

The fire was soon crackling merrily and Sandy had just started to tell a story when–

"Shhh! What was that?" whispered William.

The three stayed stock still, straining their ears for any sound.

"Ach, you're hearing things, Will," said Sandy.

At that very moment, hundreds of dark, dripping shapes closed in around the brothers. The creatures walked upright like people, but something about them was inhuman. The men were sinewy and muscular with uncommonly wide, flat feet and hands.

The women were equally unsettling; their dark eyes seemed to possess a magnetic force. Yes, it was the eyes that struck the boys the most. All the creatures had eyes of liquid jet that shone eerily in the dancing firelight. Instead of clothes, these strange folk were wrapped in velvety cloaks of sealskin. The lads were surrounded by selkies.

The selkies were shapeshifters, able to take the form of both seals and human beings. Every seventh night, they became human and walked about on two legs. The boys had heard all the myths and legends about these mystical beings but had never seen them before. The selkies spoke in their native Gaelic tongue, but the words sounded different. They were coarser, rougher – born of sea and storm.

"You meant to kill us, so we have come to seek vengeance," said one of the selkies.

What could the boys say? For it was true, and there was no use denying it when their clubs lay on the sand behind them. All they could do was stammer apologies and beg forgiveness. The selkies at the front of the crowd bent to pick up rocks and the boys started to mutter prayers. But then–

"Stop! Put those rocks down immediately."

The crowd parted for a wizened old selkie, leaning on a gnarled stick.

"You must not harm these boys," the ancient selkie commanded. "I know their father. Once, a very long time ago, I got myself tangled in some nets and could not break free. Luckily, the nets belonged to the father of these here boys. He cut me loose and showed me the meaning of true kindness. Since then, we have always respected one another. Now, take heed, young men. From this day forth, you shall never fish near our island. We are creatures of the sea, part of this ancient ecosystem. You, on the other hand, must fish floating on bits of wood, casting dreadful nets that scoop up all the fish in their path. We tried to warn you, but you wouldn't listen. Now, be gone, and don't come near Selkie Island ever again."

At once, the boys dashed away from the selkies, slipping and sliding on the dark rocks. They rowed like the wind, barely pausing to catch their breath, and ran all the way home to the croft. There they found their mother and father sitting together by the fire. The boys had never been so glad to see the familiar hearthside with its rag rug and the copper kettle that whistled gently on its hook above the fire.

"Why, whatever is it? You look pale as ghosts. You've not been a'meeting with the fairy folk have you?" asked their mother with a twinkle in her eye.

"No, Mother. We just rowed out to Selkie Island to check the fish stocks."

"How many times do I need to tell you to leave that island alone?" said their father exasperatedly.

"You're right, Father. We realise our mistake now. We should have listened all along. That island belongs to the seal folk. We'll never fish those waters again."

And nor did they.

SEEDS OF FRIENDSHIP
A story from Kazakhstan

There were once two old men called Kurai and Dau who lived together and farmed a small plot of land. They lived in a remote part of Kazakhstan on the steppe, a vast region of grassland so dry that very few things could survive on it. The friends had a few sheep and grew meagre amounts of vegetables – only just enough to live off.

Winter was always very hard on the steppe. There were no trees, so the biting winds swept through with ferocity and gnawed at the bones of the people and animals. The worst thing to happen on the steppe was the *dzhut*. In these conditions, the ground froze solidly and sometimes thick snow was heaped on top of it. This meant that the sheep couldn't get to the vegetation underneath, and some starved to death.

94

The old men were careful to look out for each other. Kurai owned the land that they lived on, and Dau was responsible for looking after the sheep. But that winter, a terrible *dzhut* hit the steppe. Dau did all that he could, but he was unable to save their sheep; all of them perished. Dau felt broken. He told Kurai that he would go to the mountains and let the elements take him. But Kurai would not hear of it.

   "You'll do nothing of the sort, Dau. I need you here and I value your company. Spring will come eventually, and then who will help me with the garden and vegetables? Who will keep me company during the long, cold nights when the only solace is the fireside and the stories of an old friend? I hereby give you ownership of the bottom half of this field."

   Well, Dau could hardly argue with this. He accepted the kind offer and the two men became joint owners of the small plot of land.

For a long time, winter was a constant and close companion to Dau and Kurai. They had almost forgotten the feeling of warm sun and could hardly recall a time when they had been able to sink their hands deep into earth that was soft and moist. But spring came at last as it always does, and the old men were able to dig again. One afternoon, as Dau was getting stuck in with his hoe, he struck something solid. Further digging revealed an old chest that looked as though it had been buried for many centuries. When Dau opened it up, he was flabbergasted. The chest was chock-full of gold!

At once, Dau took the treasure to Kurai and gave it to him.
   "You will be rich, Kurai, and nobody deserves it more than you. You are a good man."
   "But, Dau, my friend, you found the gold in your half of the field. It belongs to you and you alone."
   The two friends went on arguing about whom the gold rightfully belonged to all night. In the morning, they decided that the only way to resolve the disagreement was to find the wise man of the steppe. They told him of their predicament, and he gave it some thought.
   "The gold belongs to both of you and neither of you. Take it to the nearest city and use it to buy the best seeds available. When you return, plant these seeds and grow an orchard. It will be the orchard of friendship, available to all, no matter their class or wealth. Those who need it may rest in the shade, eat the fruit from the trees and relax in its beautiful surroundings."

The two friends thought this a very good plan indeed and set off at once for the city. They found the market and looked in vain for the seller of fruit seeds. Tired and fed up, they decided to rest for the night and begin the search again in the morning. On the way to the inn, Dau and Kurai heard a loud racket of squawking and screeching. They followed the sound and came across thousands of caged birds calling out to each other in anger and sorrow. They had been captured in the forests and were on their way to market. Their destiny was to be food on the table of wealthy people who cared only to impress their guests.

Dau and Kurai looked at each other and immediately knew what the other was thinking. The birds must be saved. Wild animals were not supposed to live under lock and key. They approached the seller and asked the price of the birds. The seller regarded them unkindly.

"You couldn't even afford one of these beautiful birds."

Dau opened the lid of the chest. "Will this be enough?"

The seller staggered back in surprise, and immediately his entire tone and manner changed.

"Sir, forgive me for my words before. I wasn't thinking straight. It would be a pleasure, no, an honour to sell you these majestic birds."

"Take the gold and release the birds," said Dau.

At once, the seller and his assistants began unlocking the cages. The birds spread their wings and took to the air joyfully, their songs no longer angry and sorrowful but melodious and cheerful. Kurai and Dau watched them soar back to their homes in the forest. They were happy that the birds were free but felt some regret for the orchard that would now never be. As they walked home, they talked of their years of strong partnership and the value of friendship. They agreed never to quarrel again.

Days later, on arriving back at their little dwelling, they were confused to see their field filled with thousands of birds. All of them were scratching about in the earth. At first, the two men thought that the birds must be digging for food, but as they got closer, they noticed that the birds were in fact planting seeds! Amazed, Dau and Kurai realised that they were the same birds that they had set free. Each held a seed in its beak. After digging a hole, the birds dropped the seed down and covered the hole over with earth. Then, with a rejoicing screech, up they flew in a blizzard of multi-coloured feathers.

Over the next few weeks, the seeds began to grow shoots that turned into little seedlings. These seedlings then became small plants, and Kurai and Dau were able to identify apple, apricot and pear trees. Their orchard was growing! The old friends tended to their saplings with such love and care that the trees became strong and healthy, able to withstand the punishing winters on the steppe. The orchard of friendship became a beacon of hope, offering shelter and solace in a barren place.

THE FOX AND THE ARMADILLO

A story from Argentina

Once upon a time, there lived two neighbours on Argentina's Pampas. The Pampas were vast plains, flat as a coin, stretching on for hundreds of thousands of miles.

The neighbours were a fox and an armadillo. They were both perfectly unaware of the other's existence.

The fox lived on an enormous farm in a wonderful position. It was sheltered and sunny, and he had to do very little work. Each season, Fox merely scattered his seeds and waited for them to grow. While he waited, he took up his favourite position under an ombú tree and lazed about in the shade all day.

The armadillo lived a very different existence. Her land was stony and dry, and although she worked a hundred times harder than the fox, she could barely grow enough food to feed her family. Every day, she spent hours in her rocky fields, doing all she could to produce half decent crops.

Meanwhile, the lazy fox grew so much food that he had enough left over to sell at market! One day, he decided to take a different route with his barrow of vegetables. This path took him past the armadillo's farm. He looked on wide-eyed at the industrious animal as she busily worked her way up and down the crops – watering, weeding, even murmuring to and caressing the plants. The fox was astonished. He had never seen anyone work so hard for so little. He continued on with his barrow of goods, but he was already concocting a plan...

On his return from the market, Fox stopped again at Armadillo's farm. This time, he called out in greeting.

"Hello, friend! I couldn't help but notice how hard you work on this barren wasteland. I admire your hard work enormously, but it doesn't seem fair that you should have to toil here while over on my land, the crops practically grow themselves! I invite you to come and share my

farm so that you too may reap the rewards of the fine conditions."

The armadillo approached hesitantly.

"It's true that my yield is very poor. All I can grow are root vegetables, such as turnips and potatoes."

"Ah, well, at my farm, I grow anything I please," boasted the fox. "In fact, I have just been to market with a whole barrowful of different vegetables and grains. It would give me great pleasure to help a neighbour in need."

"How would we divide up what I grow?" asked the armadillo.

Fox cast his eyes slyly over the armadillo's potato crop.

"Why, you may keep everything that grows above ground, and I will take whatever is left."

Now, do not be hoodwinked by this wily fox. His offer certainly sounded generous, but he was only thinking of himself and greedily hatching a plan whereby the armadillo would work for free. Potatoes grow underground. Above ground, they sprout bushy leaves that are totally inedible. Fox assumed that the armadillo only knew how to grow root vegetables, so he thought this a very safe bargain.

"It's a deal," said the armadillo.

Was she being taken for a fool?

The next day, the lazy fox did not wake till far into the afternoon. He strutted towards his fields and gleefully saw that the armadillo was already hard at work, hoeing and digging, ready to plant her seeds.

"Great work!" he called as he stretched himself out in the shade.

Before long, the little seedlings began to grow. Instead of the squat, bushy leaves of the potato, tall, slender stalks emerged from the ground. Armadillo was not a fool! Instead of potatoes, she was growing wheat. The fox didn't even notice. He was far too lazy to come and inspect the crops. Instead, he stayed under his ombú tree, dreaming of all the money he would make at market.

When the time came to harvest, Fox sauntered smugly over to the crop to reap his rewards. To his horror, he found fields of golden wheat rustling gently in the wind. The armadillo was already busy cutting down the ripe wheat and collecting it into fat bushels. Of course, as agreed, she was entitled to all that grew above ground, while Fox could take all that grew below.

"I should be finished with this field soon," said Armadillo cheerily. "Then you may collect your share."

Fox gulped. His share was hundreds of stringy roots!

"Some say I am too generous for my own good!" Fox smiled through gritted teeth. "I think next time you sow a crop, I shall take whatever grows on top and you may have what grows underground."

"As you wish," said the armadillo.

The next day, she diligently began sowing new seeds. The fox sat back, satisfied that this time he would be left with a large bounty of wheat. For the next few months, he lazed about as usual, idly dreaming and scheming. Harvest time came around again, and he prepared to go and gather his haul. Imagine his rage on finding that the armadillo had sidestepped him once again! She hummed quietly to herself as she pulled up hundreds of potatoes and placed them in her barrow.

"Won't be too much longer," she called. "I'm leaving your share of leaves in a pile here."

Fuming, the fox thought hard, determined not to be outdone.

"I'm afraid my charity has to run out sometime. For the next crop you plant, I will be allowed to take all that grows above and below ground. You may have the middle parts," Fox said.

"Fine by me," said the armadillo.

Fox skulked off, certain that this time there was no way the armadillo could outmanoeuvre him.

The season wore on, and at last the latest crop was ready to harvest. The fox arrived at the same time as the armadillo, sure that his reward was soon to be collected. But there were no wheat or potatoes in sight. Fox stared pathetically at the fields that lay before him. His gaze was greeted with rows and rows of corn. At the bottom of the plant were its roots, and at the top was the corn tassel, useful only to the bees that pollinated it. The armadillo busied herself with the middle parts. Each stalk was groaning under the weight of many ears of corn.

The fox's shocked silence soon turned to anger.

"You've swindled me three times!"

"I would never have tricked you if you hadn't tried to deceive me in the first place," said the armadillo in her calm, quiet manner.

"Next time, I shall plant my own crops and keep the produce for myself," said the fox crossly.

The armadillo eyed him shrewdly before replying.

"Perhaps, then, you have finally learnt the value of an honest day's work."

BEYOND THE STORY

Background to the Stories

The Dragon King, China
In Chinese mythology, the Dragon King is the god of rain. In ancient times, rituals were carried out to honour the Dragon King in hope of rain, such as parades and dragon dances, in which people dressed colourfully and mimicked dragon-like movements.

The Circle of Life, Kenya, Tanzania, Zanzibar
This story comes from the Swahili oral tradition. Tales were narrated or performed on special occasions and the teller would use facial expressions and body language to make them more entertaining. Swahili tales often contain a moral message.

The Banyan Tree, Tahiti
The banyan tree was considered sacred by Polynesians. It was thought that through trees, humans communicated with the gods. Sacred trees, such as the banyan, can be found at religious sites all over Polynesia.

Why Ants Live All Around, Myanmar
'Pourquoi stories' attempt to describe the origin of something. The word 'pourquoi' means 'why' in French. In early times, before we had scientific evidence, these stories tried to explain how the natural world worked. Pourquoi stories appear in many cultures.

Lighting the New Year, Norway
In Norway, during the dead of winter, there is very little natural light. For this reason, candles and firelight have always been important in Norse culture, symbolising goodness, safety, comfort and warmth.

Finding Fire, Democratic Republic of the Congo
Storytelling used to be a central part of life and culture in the Congo. Often, the stories were accompanied by music as well as call-and-response with the audience. If the teller forgot a line, it would be filled in by someone else.

The Sky Garden, Australia
This story comes from the First Nations Gamilaraay people, who originally inhabited a vast area of land in South East Australia. In their culture, the land has a spiritual value and should not be owned by humans. Rather, the land owns the people.

The Discontented Pine Tree, Denmark
During the Bronze Age, Denmark was covered by thick forests. Trees have always played an important role in Scandinavian mythology and culture: 'guardian trees' were planted next to houses in order to protect the inhabitants from bad luck.

The Corn Girl, North America
This story comes from the Native American Iroquois people. They have a great respect for nature and believe that land is not separate from humans but a living part of them. People, animals and plants all come from the same family.

Stairway to the Stars, England
The early people of England were deeply connected to the natural world and lived in harmony with the seasons. Their folklore also reflects a strong current of magic and the supernatural, inherited from paganism.

The Deer's Antlers, Greece
This is a fable by Aesop, who was a celebrated ancient Greek storyteller. Fables typically feature animal characters who can speak, and they have a moral message.

The First Woodpecker, Romania
Romania has a vast and rich natural landscape in which the majority of people used to live in small, cut-off rural communities. Ancient folk beliefs centred around a pagan religion in which a host of different elements from the natural world were worshipped.

Day Without Night, India
This story comes from the Santal people. They understand the world as a place of interconnecting relationships between creatures, nature and spirits. Santal people believe humans to be the guardians of the environment.

King and Queen of the Skies, Nigeria
The Efik people come from South West Nigeria. Traditionally, they worshipped the creator gods Abassi and Atai and prayed to forest spirits to keep their communities safe.

The Flower Thief, Syria

The Assyrians held gardens in great importance. There is evidence of domestic gardens in Mesopotamia recorded on clay tablets dating back 4,000 years.

Searching for Summer, North America
This story comes from the First Nations and Native American Wabanaki Confederacy. *Netukulimk* is a word used by the First Nations Mi'kmaq people (part of the confederacy). It means taking only what you need from the environment, rather than all that you desire.

Souls of the Earth, South Sudan
This story is from the Shilluk people who live beside the River Nile. Traditionally, they believed that all living things have a soul or spirit. This type of belief is called 'animism'.

Selkie Island, Scotland
The ancient Celts regarded the Earth itself as a goddess and the mother of all things. From Mother Earth came the spirits of mountains, rivers, trees and other elements of the natural world which were held sacred by the Celts.

Seeds of Friendship, Kazakhstan
Historically, Kazakhs were nomads. This means that they didn't live in a fixed place but travelled around. Storytellers called *akyns* would travel from camp to camp, telling tales and singing songs. Stories were designed to teach about Kazakh history or moral values.

The Fox and the Armadillo, Argentina
The Argentinian Pampas is a vast area of grassland. The eastern area is dry and barren, while the western part is lush and fertile. The Pampas was originally inhabited by nomadic indigenous peoples such as the Querandí and was later taken over by Spanish settlers.

Thinking Points

The Dragon King
Li Ching sets out with the honest intention of helping people. Why do you think he gets carried away and refuses to listen to Little Dragon?

The Circle of Life
The farmer assumes that the animals will be on his side when he begs them to save his life. What does he learn from the baboon?

The Banyan Tree
Look up at the moon tonight. Can you see why the people who first told this tale thought that giant tree roots covered its face?

Why Ants Live All Around
Ant is laughed at by the other animals for being so small. How do you think the animals feel when Ant is the only one who can help King Lion?

Lighting the New Year
Hans meets the twelve months and helps them to welcome in the new year. Can you describe the changes that happen in the natural world every month?

Finding Fire
The people are desperate to bring the warmth and light of fire into their lives. Do you think we use fire responsibly in our modern world?

The Sky Garden
The elders are unhappy living in a land without flowers. Would you notice if flowers stopped growing? If so, what would you miss about them?

The Discontented Pine Tree
The little tree tries switching her pine needles to gold, glass and maple leaves. What does she learn in the end?

The Corn Girl
The corn girl sings a song at the end of the story about the future of our planet. Do you think she is describing our generation?

Stairway to the Stars
Flora is so entranced by the sight of the stars glittering in the sky that she decides to find them. What things in nature make you feel a sense of wonder?

The Deer's Antlers
At first, the deer doesn't like his spindly legs but, in the end, he realises that they have a very useful purpose! If there's something you don't like about yourself, could you think about it in a different light?

The First Woodpecker
In the past, there was less scientific evidence to explain the world around us. Do you think that is why 'origin stories' like this were so popular?

Day Without Night
Before the creator tells the sun to set, the people live in constant daylight. How do the sun and moon help us to understand time?

King and Queen of the Skies
The moon, stars and elements all want to be more powerful than one another, but our planet requires a fine balance. When it tips, havoc and chaos reign on Earth.

The Flower Thief
The king and queen steward their garden carefully and are devastated when a rare flower is destroyed. Why is stewardship of nature so important?

Searching for Summer
Winter would like to reign over everything, but Glooskap and Summer manage to save the land from his icy grip. Why do we need different seasons?

Souls of the Earth
Juok creates people from different types of earth found all around the world. Depending on where we are from, we may look and sound very different. This variation makes humanity beautiful.

Selkie Island
The farmer's sons don't listen to his warnings in the beginning. What do they learn from their meeting with the selkies?

Seeds of Friendship
These two old friends are generous spirits, and the story highlights the importance of giving back to nature. Their orchard will live on for hundreds of years after they have died.

The Fox and the Armadillo
The fox thinks that he can trick the armadillo and get by on greed alone. The armadillo is thoughtful and resourceful; her knowledge of plants allows her to outwit the fox!

Bibliography

"The Dragon King"
"Making Rain for the Dragon," in *Chinese Folk-Tales* by William Dolby. Carreg Publishers, 2003

"The Circle of Life"
"The Lion and the Snake," in *Myths & Legends of the Swahili* by Jan Knappert. Heinemann Educational Books, 1970

"The Banyan Tree"
"The Tree in the Moon," in *The Tree in the Moon and Other Legends of Plants and Trees* by Rosalind Kerven. Cambridge University Press, 1989

"Why Ants Live All Around"
"Why Ants Live Everywhere," in *How the People Sang the Mountains Up: How and Why Stories* by Maria Leach. Viking Press, 1967

"Lighting the New Year"
"New Year's Eve," in *How the Stars Were Born: Norwegian Nature Fables, Tales and Legends* by Dan Lindholm. Henry Goulden Books, 1975

"Finding Fire"
"The Gift From a Star," in *Long Ago When the Earth Was Flat: Three Tales From Africa* by Paola Caboara Luzzato. Collins, 1980

"The Sky Garden"
"Journey to the Land of Flowers," in *The Tree in the Moon and Other Legends of Plants and Trees* by Rosalind Kerven. Cambridge University Press, 1989

"The Discontented Pine Tree"
"The Pine Tree," in *Once Upon a Time: Twenty Cheerful Tales to Read and Tell* by Rose Dobbs. Random House, 1950

"The Corn Girl"
"The Corn Maiden," in *The Tree in the Moon and Other Legends of Plants and Trees* by Rosalind Kerven. Cambridge University Press, 1989

"Stairway to the Stars"
"The Stars in the Sky," in *More English Fairy Tales* by Joseph Jacobs. Pook Press, 2018

"The Deer's Antlers"
"The Hart and the Hunter," in *The Fables of Aesop* edited by Joseph Jacobs. Dover Publications, 2002

"The First Woodpecker"
"The Woodpecker," in *The Unbroken Web: Stories and Fables* by Richard Adams. Ballantine Books, 1980

"Day Without Night"
"How Was the Moon Created?," in *Fascinating Folk Tales of India* by Swapna Dutta. Unicorn Books, 2007

"King and Queen of the Skies"
"The Man in the Moon and His Wife," in *African Folk Tales* by Yoti Lane. Peter Lunn Publishers, 1946

"The Flower Thief"
"Flowers that Vanished in the Night," in *Arab Folktales* by Inea Bushnaq. Pantheon Books, 1986

"Searching for Summer"
"How Glooskap Found the Summer," in *Native American Legends: An Anthology of Creation Myths and Origin Tales* by G.W. Mullins. Light of the Moon Publishing, 2019

"Souls of the Earth"
"Juok and the Creation of the Races," in *Myths of Creation* by Philip Freund. Washington Square Press, 1966

"Selkie Island"
"The Fisherman and his Sons," in *The Broonies, Silkies & Fairies: Travellers' Tales* by Duncan Williamson. Canongate Books, 1985

"Seeds of Friendship"
"The Friendship Orchard," in *Stories of the Steppes: Kazakh Folktales* by Mary Lou Masey. David McKay Company, 1968

"The Fox and the Armadillo"
"The Greedy Fox," in *Latin American Tales from the Pampas to the Pyramids of Mexico* by Genevieve Barlow. Rand McNally, 1966

"Tell me the facts and I'll learn.
Tell me the truth and I'll believe.
But tell me a story and it will
live in the heart forever."

— Native American proverb

THE
END